S0-AFG-532

SARI OF THE GODS

SARI OF THE GODS

STORIES BY

G.S. SHARAT CHANDRA

COFFEE HOUSE PRESS MINNEAPOLIS

Rep. 2014/09

WITHDRAWN

COPYRIGHT © 1998 by G.S. Sharat Chandra
ILLUSTRATION © 1997 Douglas Oudekerk
COVER/BOOK DESIGN by Kelly Kofron
BACK COVER PHOTOGRAPH by Anjana Chandra

Acknowledgments are due to the following periodicals and anthologies where some of these stories first appeared: "Sari of the Gods" in *Female* (Singapore); "Dot Busters" and "Seams & Desires" in *New Letters;* "Maya" in *Swallow's Tale;* "The Lady Chieftain" in *Green Mountains Review;* "Jamal the Constable" in *Winter's Tales* (England); "The Holy Wristwatch" and "Encounter" in *London Magazine;* "The Elephant Stop" in *Overland* (Australia); "Reincarnation" in *These and Other Lands;* "Bhat's Return" in *Missouri Short Fiction;* "Selves," "Iyer's Hotel," and "This Time Goat; Next Time Man" in *Stories;* "Demon" in *The International Quarterly.* Several of these stories have been anthologized in *The Short Story International; Writing Fiction* (Little, Brown); *The Shock of Being Foreign* (Intercultural Press); and *Face to Face* (Houghton Mifflin).

Coffee House Press is supported in part by a grant provided by the Minnesota State Arts Board, through an appropriation by the Minnesota State Legislature, and in part by a grant from the National Endowment for the Arts. Significant support has also been provided by The McKnight Foundation; Lannan Foundation; Jerome Foundation; Target Stores, Dayton's, and Mervyn's by the Dayton Hudson Foundation; General Mills Foundation; St. Paul Companies; Butler Family Foundation; Honeywell Foundation; Star Tribune/Cowles Media Company; James R. Thorpe Foundation; Dain Bosworth Foundation; Pentair, Inc.; the Helen L. Kuehn Fund of The Minneapolis Foundation; the law firm of Schwegman, Lundberg, Woessner & Kluth, P.A.; and many individual donors. To you and our many readers across the country, we send our thanks for your continuing support.

Coffee House Press books are available to the trade through our primary distributor, Consortium Book Sales & Distribution, 1045 Westgate Drive, Saint Paul, MN 55114. For personal orders, catalogs, or other information, write to: Coffee House Press, 27 North Fourth Street, Suite 400, Minneapolis, MN 55401.

Printed in Canada

LIBRARY OF CONGRESS CIP INFORMATION
Sharat Chandra, G.S., 1935 –
    Sari of the gods : stories / by G.S. Sharat Chandra.
      p.   cm.
    ISBN 1-56689-071-3 (pb : alk. paper)
    1. Title.
    PR9499.3.S45S27 1998
    823—dc21

97-43200
CIP

10 9 8 7 6 5 4 3 2 1

WITHDRAWN

GOSHEN COLLEGE LIBRARY
GOSHEN, INDIANA

CONTENTS

HERE
1

THERE
2

NEITHER HERE NOR THERE
3

for my daughters
SHALINI AND ANJANA

may their lives be filled with little miracles of human insight

1

HERE

Sari of the Gods

One of the things that Prapulla had insisted on was to have a place waiting for them in New York where other Indian immigrants lived. She had worried a great deal over this sudden change in her life. First, there was her fear of flying over Mount Everest—a certain intrusion over Lord Shiva's territory. Then the abrupt severance of a generation of relationships and of life in an extended family.

She had spent many a restless night. In daylight, she'd dismiss her nightmares as mere confusions of a troubled mind and set herself to conquer her problems as she faced them, like the educated and practical woman that she was. If anything happened to the transgressing jet, she would clutch her husband and child to her breasts and plummet with at least a partial sense of wholeness to whatever ocean the wrath of the god would cast her. She would go down like those brave, legendary sea captains in the history books and movies. But moving over to the West where one lived half the year like a monk in a cave because of the weather was something she couldn't visualize. Besides, how was she going to manage her household without the maid-servant and her stalwart mother-in-law? To be left alone in a strange apartment all day while Shekar went to work was a recurring fear. She had heard that in New York City, even married women wore miniskirts or leather slacks and thought nothing of getting drunk, not to mention their sexual escapades in parks or parked automobiles. But cousin Manjula, who had returned from the States, was most reassuring. "All that is nonsense! Women there are just like women here! Only they have habits and customs quite different from ours. There are hundreds of Indian families in New York. Once you've acclimatized yourself to the country, you'll find it hard to sit and brood. You may run into families from Bangalore in the same apartment, who knows!"

Prapulla liked the apartment house as soon as she saw some women wearing saris in the lobby. It was Shekar who looked distraught at the sight of Indian faces. In the time it took them to travel from the airport to the apartment, he had seen many of his brown brethren on the city streets, looking strange and out of place. Now he dreaded being surrounded by his kind, ending up like them building little Indias in the obscure corners of New York. He wasn't certain what Prapulla thought about it. She was always quiet on such subjects. Back in India, she was a recluse when it came to socializing and on the few occasions they had entertained foreigners at the firm, she would seek the nearest sofa as a refuge and drop her seven yards of brocade at anchor. She left the impression of being a proper Hindu wife, shy, courteous, and traditional.

En route to New York on the jumbo, Shekar had discreetly opened up the conversation about what she'd wear once they were in America. At the mention of skirts, she had flared up so defiantly he had to leave the seat. For Prapulla, it was not convenience but convention that made the difference. She had always prized her saris, especially on the occasions when she wore her wedding sari with its blue, hand-spun silk and its silver border on which images of the gods had been embroidered. There were times when she had walked into a crowded room where others were dressed differently and she had relished the sudden flush of embarrassment on their faces at her exquisite choice of wear.

The first day of their new life went quite smoothly. When Shekar returned from the office, she was relieved to hear that all had gone well and that he had made friends with two of his American colleagues.

Shekar described them. Don Dellow had been in the firm for fifteen years and was extremely pleasant and helpful. Jim Dorsen and his wife Shirley had always wanted to visit India and shared great interest in the country and its culture.

"I bought them lunch at the corner deli, you know, and you should've seen their faces when I asked for corned beef on rye!" Shekar chuckled.

It was during that weekend that her husband suggested they ought to invite the Dellows and the Dorsens for dinner so she could meet and get to know the wives. Prapulla shrugged her shoulders. It was so soon. She was still unaccustomed to walking into the sterilized supermarkets where you shopped like a robot with a pushcart, where the products lay waiting like cheese in a trap, rather than beseeching you from the stalls of the vendors and merchants in the bazaars and markets of home. The frozen vegetables, the canned fruits and spices, the chicken chopped into shapes that were not its own but of the plastic, all bothered her. Besides, everything had a fixed price tag.

But Shekar had not complained about her cooking yet. He was so busy gabbing and gulping, she wasn't even sure he knew what was on the plate. Then Shekar walked in from the office on Thursday and announced he had invited his friends for dinner on Saturday. "They both accepted with great delight. It's rather important I develop a strong bond with them." Prapulla pulled out a pad and started the shopping list. Shekar began to ask her what she'd wear but changed his mind.

The Dorsens arrived first. Shirley Dorsen introduced herself and immediately took a liking to Prapulla. The Dellows, caught in traffic, came late. Judy Dellow was a lean Spanish woman in her late twenties. She wore a velvet dress with lace cuffs and asked for bourbon. The living room filled with the aroma of spices. In the background, Subbalakshmi recited on the stereo.

"What sort of music is this?" Jim asked, looking somewhat sullen. He had just finished his drink. Shirley was on her fourth.

"Karnatak music," explained Prapulla. "Subbalak-shmi is *the* soprano of South Indian music. She sings mostly devotional songs and lyrics."

"Sounds rather strange and off key to me," said Jim shaking his head in dismay. He sang for the church choir on Sundays.

Shekar announced dinner. He had set the wine glasses next to the handloomed napkins as he had seen in *Good Housekeeping*. As soon as everyone was seated, he abruptly got up. "Gee! I forgot to pour the wine!" he despaired. When he returned, he held an opaque bottle with a long German name.

"What kind of wine is it?" asked Jim.

"The best German Riesling there is!" replied Shekar with authority.

"My, you do know your wine!" said Shirley, impressed.

"Like a book!" quipped Prapulla.

"It's a misconception," Shekar continued hastily, "that French wines are the best. Germans actually mastered the art of wine-making long before the French. Besides, you can't beat a German Riesling to go with Indian food."

"Excellent!" said Jim.

Shekar filled the glasses, apologizing again for not having filled them beforehand. "You see, good wine has to be chilled right," he added, avoiding Prapulla's unflinching stare. They began to eat. Shirley attacked everything, mumbling superlatives between mouthfuls. Shekar kept a benevolent eye on the plates and filled them as soon as they were empty. Prapulla sat beaming an appropriate smile. When everyone had their fill, Prapulla got up for dessert.

"Is it going to be one of the exotic Indian sweets?" asked Shirley, looking unappeased.

"Of course," exclaimed Shekar.

Prapulla returned from the kitchen with Pepperidge Farm turnovers. "Sorry, I had an accident with the jamoons," she said meekly.

"Don't worry dear. Turnovers do perfectly well," said Shirley, giving her an understanding look.

Shekar had placed a box of cigars on the coffee table. As they all sat, he offered it to his guests, who waved it away in preference to their own crumpled packages of Salems. Don and Jim talked about a contract the firm had lost. A junior engineer from Bombay who used to work for the firm had bungled it. They asked Shekar if he knew the man. Shekar stiffened in his chair. When he pressed for details, they veered the conversation away from the topic to compliment him on his choice of brandy.

Prapulla entered carrying a tray of coffee mixed with cream and sugar, just like back home. Subbalakshmi coughed, cleared her throat, and strummed the veena in prayer.

Judy raved about Prapulla's sari. Prapulla, momentarily saved from embarrassment over the coffee, began to explain the ritual importance of the wedding sari. She pulled the upper part from her shoulder and spread it on the table, describing the silver border with the embroidered legend of the creation of the universe. The different avatars of Lord

Shiva and the demons he killed while on earthly mission gleamed under the light. Her favorite vignette depicted Shiva drinking the poison emitted by the sea serpent with which the universe was churned from the ocean. The craftsman had even put a knot of gold at Shiva's neck to indicate the poison the god had held in his throat—a sheer triumph of skill!

"With the exception of Shiva as the begging ascetic, the sari maker has woven all the other avatars. This blank space on the border is perhaps left to challenge our imagination!" mused Prapulla. Shirley, with a snifter full of brandy, leaned from her chair for a closer look. The brandy tipped. "Oh no!" screamed everyone. Judy ran into the kitchen for a towel, but the alcohol hissed like a magical serpent over the sari spreading its poisonous hood. The silver corroded immediately and the avatars, disfigured and mutilated, almost merged. Prapulla sat dazed, just staring at her sari. The silence was unbearable. Jim puffed on his pipe like a condemned man. Judy, after trying valiantly to wipe the brandy, bent her head over her hand. Shirley looked red, as if she was either going to scream or giggle. Shekar came to the rescue:

"Don't worry. I know a way I can lift the smudges. It's nothing!"

No one believed him. Prapulla abruptly got up and excused herself.

"I guess we had better be leaving," said Don looking at his watch. "I have to drive the baby-sitter home and she lives three traffic jams away!"

Shekar hurried to the closet for their coats. "I hope you enjoyed the dinner," he said meekly, piling the coats over his shoulder.

Prapulla appeared at the door in a different sari. She seemed to have collected herself and felt bad about everyone leaving so soon. "You know, my husband is right. I've already dipped the sari's border in the lotion. It'll be as good as new by morning," she said.

They shook hands and Shirley hugged Prapulla and rocked her. "I'll call you, dear, let me know how it comes off!" she whispered drunkenly and backed into her coat like a trained animal.

Prapulla stood at the door with one hand on her stomach, and as the guests disappeared down the elevator she banged the door shut and ran into the bedroom. She remembered the day she had shopped for the sari. It had been a week before her wedding. The entire family had gone to the silk bazaar and spent the day looking for the perfect one. They had at last found it in the only hand-spun sari shop in the market. The merchant had explained that the weaver who had knitted the gods into its border had died soon after, taking his craft with him. This was his last sari, his parting gift to some lucky bride. "You modern young people may not believe in old wives' tales, but I know that he was a devotee of Shiva. People say the Lord used to appear for him!" the merchant had said.

She sobbed into her shoulders. Where was she going to find a replacement? How was she ever going to explain the tragedy to her family? A wedding sari, selected by the bride, became her second self, the sail of her destiny, the roof that protected her and her offspring from evil. She rushed to Ratri's room to make sure that no mythical serpent or scorpion had already appeared over her daughter's head.

She could hear Shekar washing the dishes in the kitchen and turning on the sinkerator that gurgled like a demon with its gulletful of leftovers. She fought the impulse to make sure that Shekar had not fallen into it. It was not really Shirley's fault. It was the brandy that Prapulla's "Americanized" husband kept pouring into her glass. He was so obsequious, lavishing food and liquor that they could scarcely afford on people that were yet to be called friends. He had drunk more than he should have, as if to prove that he held his liquor well enough to win points for promotion. Who had really wanted brandy? Shekar had clumsily turned the picture of Napoleon on the bottle toward his guests, but surely it must have been a demon who despised her or was sent to convey the gods' displeasure at her mixed company, her expatriatism.

She grew tired of her mind's hauntings. There was no way to change the events or turn back now. When Ratri grew up, Prapulla would cut the sari and make a dress for her. She'd write to her mother-in-law and send money for a special puja at the temple. Tonight, there was nothing left to do but sleep.

In her dream, she saw her own funeral. Four priests carried her on bamboo. The family walked behind. Shekar, dressed in traditional dhoti, walked ahead with the clay vessel of hot coals with which he'd kindle the first spark of fire. The procession moved briskly to the crematory grounds. A pyre was built and her corpse, decked with her favorite flowers, was laid on top. Someone tied the border of the sari firmly to a log. The bereaved went around chanting the necessary hymns and the priests sprinkled holy water over her. Suddenly she was ablaze. She felt nothing but an intense heat around her. The flames did not seem to touch her. She pinched herself. She was not on the pyre but was standing with her family. It was her wedding sari wrapped around a giant bottle of brandy that was burning! Inside the bottle a demon danced, spitting fire. The avatars slowly uncurled from the silver border like an inflated raft and ascended the smoke. They were all in miniature, fragile in their postures and luminous. The brandy in the bottle foamed and swirled like an ocean. The demon raved in its ring of fire. Prapulla screamed. One of the uncles gently touched her on the arm and said, "Do not be alarmed. The demon points its tongue upward. The gods have flown to their proper heaven."

When she woke from the nightmare, Shekar was soundly snoring next to her. The sky outside hung in a spent, listless gray. She could see a haze of light in back of a skyscraper. Dawn would soon brim the horizon of her new world with neither birds nor the song of priests in the air. She sat in the dark of the living room with the sari on her lap, caressing its border absentmindedly. A brittle piece broke and fell.

Dot Busters

When Radha returned from the grocery store where three white youths, calling themselves Dot Busters, ridiculed her kumkum, Dev said, "We must simply tolerate such misunderstandings." He was speaking aloud to himself. The curious often asked him questions about Indian customs that he felt most uncomfortable explaining.

The miscreants who had harassed Radha hung around the neighborhood supermarket. They worked part-time in the mall, and these days the sari-clad women shopping in the neighborhood provided them much amusement. Radha felt alienated from most of the new Indians who arrived from different parts of the country, but at times it was comforting to see them in the aisles of whiteness or to hear a familiar phrase in Hindi followed by a run of abrupt English, as if they were all practicing. But try as they might, their accents dented the words like coconuts falling from a tree onto the hood of a brand-new American car.

When Radha pushed the cart out of the exit door, the Dot Buster with the barrel chest and GOTCHA t-shirt—apparently the gang's leader—approached her as if he wished to lend a hand.

"Hey, lady, why do you wear that thing on your forehead? Your husband throw darts at it?"

Radha looked back through the door at the store manager, who kept his head bent over the calculator. The girl who had checked Radha out was close enough to see but acted as if she enjoyed what was happening. Radha shook her head to drive away such thoughts.

The gang leader pushed the cart through the parking lot, swerving like a drunken driver. Grapes and bread on top of the bags shivered before they fell. "Gee, I'm sorry. What's this?" he asked holding a carton of buttermilk with two fingers, sniffing the top of it with disgust. "You drink this shit?" It plopped against the curb. The gang leader feigned surprise and looked at her. She remained calm, hoping the fear didn't show.

It was simply a matter of time, a matter of letting him do whatever he wanted until he lost interest and let go of the cart. *Groceries could be replaced*, she told herself. Her forehead throbbed. She needed to think of something else to keep from losing control.

Seeing that he wasn't getting any response, the youth shoved the cart against the curb, failing to upturn it and left.

Radha took charge, placed the bags inside the car and shut the trunk. Getting in, she started the engine and backed the car out of the parking lot. Only when she entered the main street did the tires screech, but not before the buttermilk carton hurtled like a missile to thud and explode on the rear window, its contents splattering across the glass. She sped, hoping for a patrol car to spot and stop her. She discovered that she had detoured into unfamiliar lanes that seemed to turn into each other. She glanced at the dark, milky patches on the rear window as if they were telling her something, and hoped she could find a car wash. But the maze of turns and detours arrowed back to a familiar traffic light where an Indian woman pulled up beside her in the next lane. Mesmerized, Radha watched the woman caress the kumkum dot on her own face in the mirror, the very thing Radha felt so nervous about. Indian women wore the traditional round red mark to signify they were Hindu—and suddenly this symbol of belonging had marked her as an outsider.

"We must call the supermarket manager," she said, oblivious to what Dev was saying.

"Then what? He's going to ask for your name and telephone number. Those thugs will know you must be the one who complained. Do you want that?"

Radha hung up. By the time she placed the groceries in the refrigerator, she felt numb and distant, as if it had all happened to someone else, like her friend Poonam.

"If you see a vermilion apparition in sari moving toward you in the midst of whiteness, it's Poonam," friends joked.

"Poonam creates traffic jams in the shopping aisles. People can't tell if she's real or a statue moving on its own feet," her husband exclaimed often.

But Poonam heeded no one. "Why should I change?" Poonam would ask when others questioned. "I'm an Indian woman living in America. That doesn't mean I should give up my habits. I dress the way I want, go out when I want, where I want!"

Even before the Dot Busters harassed Radha, saris and kumkum dots had become a festering annoyance among some shoppers, while security guards suspected it to be some sort of a ploy, like the roving bands of gypsies that occasionally hit their supermarkets and walked away with things hidden under heavy robes. Only a year or two after immigrating, many Indians bought expensive cars and houses. How could they do it, wrapped in shower curtains?

Then the incident at Poonam's apartment appeared in the newspapers. The Dot Busters, until now simply a nuisance around shopping areas, had found their way to Poonam's apartment, after pestering her earlier at a movie complex. Poonam had gone to see the movie dressed elaborately as it was a festival day. Her kumkum dot had glittered with extra helpings of stardust. The Dot Busters were there, and after the movie the gang leader pushed her against the railing. Poonam's husband asked him to apologize, but the youth pretended not to understand a single word and, with a shove, tripped the husband. Poonam yelled an unexpected obscenity and the gang leader left, making signs like a mafioso. Poonam and her shaken-up husband returned to their apartment. Among friends, they gathered to celebrate the festival and forgot the incident. An hour or so after the friends left, there was a knock and Poonam's husband, thinking it might be a returning guest, opened the door. Before he could say "Hare Ram!" the gang leader pushed him aside and threw acid on Poonam's forehead. His accomplice punched and kicked Poonam's husband until he was unconscious. Somehow, Poonam managed to reach the phone before fainting. Weeks later, when Poonam left the hospital, she vowed not to show her forehead to anyone outside the house.

+≻══◄+

Like ants facing an invasion of termites, Indian women reacted. If they went out in the evenings, it was with a male escort. Their foreheads were bare while they shopped or ran errands. But weeks passed, and as if burning Poonam's forehead and getting away with it were enough, the Dot Busters were nowhere to be seen. Indian women gradually returned the dots to their foreheads and felt relieved.

But the incident haunted Radha. She became afraid of everything that proclaimed her identity, and for a Hindu woman there were many that openly made such claims. If the dot was a visible symbol for attack, what would be next—the sari? In nightmares, the

Indian past mixed with the American present. She was drawn by the tip of her sari through old Indian streets by American movie gangsters who held court by a swimming pool and stripped her like Draupadi. But unlike Draupadi's sari, which after being blessed by Lord Krishna kept growing forever, Radha's sari dissolved, leaving her naked and screaming.

During the daytime she spent hours in front of the mirror puzzling over her makeup, playing with her dot, reducing it to a flimsy speck or enlarging it to the size of a planet. She wore Levi's for jogging and hurried past anyone who stopped to look. Hating herself for such behavior, she'd drive for hours or go to the park and walk on the well-lit trail, secretly daring someone to think of an assault. She began wearing a metal claw, a souvenir from her college days in India. Thus armored, she was amazed by this half-wish for confrontation. She'd caress the claw on her left hand. Similar to the one the warrior-king Shivaji used against a Moghul invader to escape treachery, it looked like rings on one's fingers while the fist was clenched, its teeth safely curved inside the palm. Heavy and reassuring, it was something to believe in. When angry, she wished for a chance to use it. But when nothing much happened, the claw turned burdensome and clumsy. Besides, to think that one had to be armed everyday like an avenging knight wasn't normal.

As if destiny created burdens in pairs, Dev needed bypass surgery and Radha discovered she was pregnant. But a friend helped Radha through these crises. Gloria, who had moved to the neighborhood, was a striking, auburn-haired, trim-figured Yale graduate, divorced, with a four-year-old daughter, Robin. Lesbian by choice, her lover Marge was an English professor from Bar Harbor who spent her holidays in New Jersey. Radha found Glo's open and uninhibited style endearing. Dev was aghast, but he had angina to worry about.

"Now there are two of you—a dot-dabbling Indian and a Yankee lesbian. I wouldn't be surprised if someone burned a cross on our lawn," he groaned.

"Fear has no gender, or does it?" asked Radha. For that Dev had no answer.

It was this clarity of logic that bonded Radha and Glo. "We mustn't stop doing things we feel strongly about just because we're harassed and intimidated. I love your kumkum and you shouldn't let male bums scare you from wearing it," Glo said.

Soon Glo was a comrade, wearing plastic dots on her forehead along with buffalo horn earrings. The dot and the earrings matched her buoyant personality.

"You look like an Indian princess in a safari outfit stepping out of a Rolls Royce to pose for Samsara," Radha would comment. Glo began reading Sanskrit lyrics and experimenting with Indian spices, seduced by their exotic smells.

One afternoon while wearing dots, they went on a trial run to a shopping center.

"Let's see what they'll do. You've got claws, I've got feet," Glo said lifting her narrow, curved foot, swinging it in a hypnotic arc like a Shaolin combatant.

A few shoppers stared oddly, but no one bothered them. Before they could widen their taunting to all shopping malls, however, Dev suffered a stroke.

Radha had no time for anything but the house and the hospital. Glo took over. She was such a comfort to come home to. With a glass of wine, listening to Robin narrate the day's events at grade school, Radha dreamed of the day when her own child would be in grade school.

When the baby was born, it was Glo who sat and held Radha's hand during the delivery. It was as if the baby was their own.

It became obvious that Dev wouldn't recover. Once in a while, he wrote messages to Radha on a pad. In one he suggested that Radha should think of remarrying so their newborn son would have a healthy father.

"Such a noble man," sighed Glo.

After Sai was born and Dev passed away, the years went by in a blur. Radha had to jog her memory to remember special events. As Dev had wished, his funeral was taken care of expeditiously by professionals. Dev donated most of his healthy organs. Fully tranquilized, Radha met those who came, thanked them and, escorted by Glo and her lover Marge, watched Dev buried in a small cemetery. Days went by and once in a while she woke up from a deep sleep thinking she was late for a visit at his bedside. Birthdays, picnics, the times they went boating, and the many small things that take over one's time day by day gained a normalcy and routine in which she recovered her balance. But a cry remained deep within her, and she often dreamed of someone with a face intimate yet unrecognizable, weeping. It was a cry now searching for something lost.

In her practical moods she recognized the conflict between her need and her reluctance to break away from all that made her what she was—a woman with ties to the past who needed to break from them, befitting the life she had chosen in America. But the dense past clung like cockleburs in the folds of her Levi's. One by one she had to take them off. It wasn't easy.

It was winter and Marge hadn't been able to get away for Christmas. Glo and Radha took care of Robin and Sai, who now shared the same bedroom. On Christmas Eve, in their separate and lonely despair, Radha and Glo drank enough to fall into bed together. When they began kissing, it was only in drunken friendliness, but soon they were passionate and wanting. In the morning, waking up in each other's arms, they were happy.

Glo wrote about this new development to Marge, who wasn't the jealous type. Radha wasn't certain that falling into a triangle was desirable. At times she felt terribly depressed and unsure. Her Indian ancestry reared its head to whisper that Sai needed a father. Furthermore, on some nights Radha couldn't get rid of her desire for the male body.

"It's my background, like my insistence on wearing the dot," Radha said to Glo. "I just don't feel whole. Somehow my upbringing seems to stick in my soul. I must remold it, even if it be by a desperate revolt."

Glo assured her she would, by and by. Everything Glo clearly rationalized made sense at the moment. But when alone, Radha felt hesitant and unsure, as if she had bifurcated into distinct halves, one seeking the new, the other longing to linger in tranquil waters. Marge and Glo, having fought their own battles of the will, understood. They shared each other fearlessly and they were pliant and harmonious, as if the secret to domestic bliss had simply resolved itself in a triangle of yin. Still, Radha needed force, a plan not of her own to propel her. Radha's traditional Indian friends, afraid to verbally confront her, gossiped and made it clear with their eyes that they didn't like her new ways. How dare she betray Dharmic code, the laws of Indian womanhood? They felt it imperative to somehow restrain her soul from further damage.

It was New Year's Eve and Glo and Marge were away when the telephone rang and a friend asked Radha to the celebrations at the temple and then to a party. Ropy, her Indian classmate who had stayed in India and had become famous, was visiting. He wished to meet her. His paintings were selling in SoHo.

Nowadays Radha felt at home in the anonymity of the American Levi's and shirt. She wasn't going to change just to appease Asian critics. She opened the kumkum box and chose a large crimson dot, and for some odd reason slid the Shivaji claw over her left fingers.

Very early in the morning, she stopped at the grocery store, having forgotten about the Dot Busters. The parking lot was almost deserted. In fact, she didn't even feel like a target, so that when a couple of youths parked next to her in a car with the radio full blast, she thought nothing of it. She returned holding Sai by one hand and a bunch of tulips in the other, when suddenly one of the boys pinned her against the car. He pressed her legs apart, working his groin while his buddy kept a grip on Sai.

"Let go of my son, you bastard," she cried.

"Name's Tom. Suck me first," said her assailant.

She had to free her left hand. "Okay, but you're holding my hand," she said. She could feel the youth's bulging balls.

"Hold onto your flowers. I like them there when I come," he said, letting go of her left hand. Radha pressed on his zipper and fiddled with it while Tom winked at his buddy.

"I won't do it unless my son's in my car," she said.

"Let the bastard go. Maybe he'd like to watch his mom," yelled Tom, and Radha motioned to Sai to get into the car.

She fiddled with Tom's zipper some more while he pushed her head down. Then, fondling Tom's organ, she opened her palm and thrust the claw upward until she could feel it sink, spraying hot, sticky blood between her fingers. Tom jerked back, holding his penis in horror as it dripped.

Radha lifted the kumkum dot from her forehead and smacked it on Tom's.

"Show your friends what a dot can do!" she screamed, planning her getaway quickly before either Tom or his friend recovered from the momentary shock that her sudden and unexpected response threw them into. Quickly, she got inside the car, threw the tulips on the back seat, then wiped her hand. She threw the soiled tissue paper on the street as she drove. Sai sat motionless for a while, then he tried the claw on his fingers where they hung absurdly loose. He smiled at her as a boy would at a father.

"Would you like to go fishing?" she asked. A quiet strength possessed her, the kind that grows on its own.

"Yeah," said Sai, wide eyed.

"Don't say anything at the party." She gently ruffled Sai's hair. "Soon I'll take you to Long Island Sound or Atlantic City, wherever the fish bite hard."

Seams & Desires

"Come look, I killed her!" Madhu said. In his right hand he held a gleaming pair of scissors. There were no bloodstains on the blades or on his clothes. He was wearing his Nehru jacket, the one he had brought with him to this country. After leaving Bombay, his jet landed at the Heathrow Airport in London where, struck by the frenzy of lights and booming intercom voices, he had sat paralyzed in the lounge while his companions hopped around the airport boutiques. When his American departure was announced, one of his fellow passengers coaxed him into a shop full of women's clothing. Madhu, afraid of the permanent scowl on the face of the salesgirls, picked what he now held in his hands. The Nehru jacket, stitched by an Indian tailor, was crumpled as if he never took it off. The pearl buttons on its collar were dangling from threadbare anchors. The last time I had seen him, I was struck by his emaciated body, but now he looked as if he were the hunger artist himself, the shapeless jacket hanging over his shoulders like a protective shell out of which his neck peeked in fear. Only his voice remained human.

Let me recount our first meeting with Madhu, several months before. Sheila and I met him at our housewarming party. He lived upstairs and our landlady assured us that he'd be no trouble. "I hate to ask him to leave, because he's such a helpless person," she explained. He had been living in Kansas City ever since he came to this country. Sheila had fallen in love with the house, though we had to be content occupying only the lower part until we could afford a mortgage. This was our third year of marriage; we had survived a troubled period, and this was our attempt to see if the seasoned walls of a house, not the trembling partitions of an apartment, held answers to domestic bliss. In our past bouts of discontent, apartment after apartment had lashed at us with inbred spirits of spite. This was our getaway from their boxed pursuit.

For the housewarming, we invited Madhu out of politeness. Sheila thought it'd be a worthy gesture. We met him while we were moving in and exchanged a few courtesies. He mentioned his troubles as a new arrival and then disappeared. The landlady told us he had lived in the rooms upstairs for two years, and would move when the house was sold. I met him again when he knocked on the door, wearing his Nehru jacket. Seeing that I was also from India, he mentioned his troubles as a recent immigrant and then disappeared from the party.

Once we settled in, which took us a couple of weeks, Sheila resumed her old habit of running around in her negligée. Since the laundry room in this Victorian mansion was at the back of the hallway, our doors stayed open. I don't know whether it was the charm of the early sun shining through the high windows overlooking the ravine to the east of us or the spacious feel of the living room with its lofty beams and wooden archways, but I looked forward to sitting for a long while on the sofa with the newspaper while Sheila roamed in and out of the doors, humming to the symphonies on the stereo. The slants of light played on her body as she moved, distracting me. I secretly relished my voyeurism and kept my eyes at least partly on the headlines. If Sheila caught me gawking, she'd stop and self-consciously reach for the bathrobe on the back of the kitchen door.

I liked the largeness the house gave us. Its walls hung back from our bodies as if surrendering to us the choice to be what we wished. I had never enjoyed doors this way before, and I was certain Sheila felt the same way, for she roamed fearlessly, half naked. There was only one recurring worry. What if our upstairs neighbor surprised us with a sudden intrusion? Luckily, he never did.

A few days later, however, Sheila announced she had accosted Madhu.

"I caught him on the stairs this morning. He apologized for leaving our party without telling us. He's quite shy."

"Thank God shyness is still a virtue," I snapped, perhaps meaning other things that were on my mind.

Sheila was used to the strange connections I made in my head between happenings and imaginings. This was a writer's way, I told her in our first apartment, when I sold our inherited bed to fit a desk into the bedroom. Nothing much came of my sarcasm. In this house, we could fall asleep without having to face each other with clear meanings.

Some days later, we were shopping for records. In the foreign section I discovered a concerto by Shankar, who had invented the double violin. We took it home and turning the stereo to full blast, sipped a bottle of Granduca Barolo. In between ragas, there was a knock on the door. It was Madhu.

"Wonderful South Indian music! May I borrow it next time only?" he asked, bowing his hands in greeting. Before I could say anything, he turned his back and closed the door.

"Why didn't you ask him in?" Sheila queried, aslant on the carpet in her green silk sari embroidered with swans gliding up and down her low-cut blouse. I shrugged and let Shankar play. After we made love, I took the record upstairs. Madhu didn't respond to my knock. I heard some voices and left the record at his doorstep.

I told Sheila about the voices.

"Maybe he was talking in his sleep," she replied.

Next evening, the record was back at my door with a note. "Thank you. Bought one for oneself."

I was glad. Perhaps now he'd engage himself with loud music and break the roomy silence in which he lived. I had no idea what he did indoors. His windows were heavily draped. Sheila told me that he came from Kerala, a South Indian state known for its socialists and witchcraft. He worked at the Oriental Bazaar on Westport, a local habitat for miscellaneous mystics of the town, where red-haired girls smoked pot and burned incense to the blare of Heavy Metal. Even there, he was hardly known. The girls loved it, I guess—the oriental inscrutability of his name, which he refused to explain. Now with a new record, he might invite fellow initiates to party—at least the red-head with the impish smile and permanently dazed look. Maybe he had already; those whispers I had heard, the two distinct voices, the inaudible softness of intimacy. He was changing, I was sure. Maybe it was our presence downstairs, or maybe it was the record. I'm sure he played it. Sheila thought I was hearing things in my head, as usual.

I admire people who can leave a country like a snake shedding its skin to blend into a new landscape, oblivious to their original identity. I've met one or two Indians who changed first names such as Vishnu or Hari to Vic or Harry. The ecstasy of a new beginning in middle age was theirs. I've envied them and at times wished I could be like them. I've changed and I've adapted to a new life, but whenever I'm surrounded by a crowd, its whiteness suffocates me. I move conscious of my self and body as if misplaced.

Sheila is quite the opposite. She's quick, vigorous, enticing in the company of people, as if she draws an energy to unsheathe her ebullience. She lets her hair down and fills the place with laughter. It only makes me nervous and on guard, for I suspect that everyone is staring at us as a mismatch. If I complain to Sheila, soon she too turns sullen and watchful. In the past, I used to blame it all on apartment life, how it restricted one's consciousness. Sometimes, especially when the day brought good news from an editor, we romped with new-found gaiety and recklessness. But always something followed—a chance remark with unintended bite or sarcasm, a mindless flirtation, a crowded exchange; we'd retreat from each other. Life is such a blend of odds and ends. When we are depressed or hurt, it doesn't matter whether the wounds are real or imagined.

Let me get back to Madhu, the enigma. Until this night, we saw him only briefly, exchanged smiles or greetings, but that was all. Now, he loomed in front of me with terrible urgency.

I followed Madhu upstairs. He was leaping the steps, snipping his weapon nervously, muttering to himself in Malayalam. I kept a step or two behind, just in case. Sheila was out for the evening, and I was glad. If Madhu had murdered someone upstairs, it was better that I handle it. If chance permitted, it was best to disarm him, tie him up somehow, and call the police. Madhu was drunk and off balance as he climbed the steps, so it would be easy. If I saw a body, I would grab Madhu from behind. Until then, I would treat this as a joke. Madhu opened the door and stepped aside to let me enter.

Since the record incident, I had been hearing footsteps and voices more and more often. One night, I
crept up after hearing the shrill voice of a woman trying to sing, wishing it was the redhead from the
bazaar. But the voices turned out to be men speaking
Malayalam, switching now and then to English. If the
redhead was there, she hardly spoke, but I thought I
heard bangles. Next day I visited the bazaar to see the
redhead so smoked out she mistook me for Madhu
and tried to hug me. Her mouth smelled of mint
leaves. She was soft and quite limp in my arms. She
must've been upstairs with Madhu the previous night,
I told Sheila later.

"Last night while you slept, our friend upstairs had
an orgy."

"Good for him." Sheila tossed the salad.

"It was the redhead from the bazaar, maybe two or
three other men."

"How do you know it was the redhead?" The salad
bowl was suddenly silent.

"I smelled a lot of pot."

Sheila looked at me, screwing up her eyes with that
old disbelieving look.

"What's the redhead's name?" There was undis-
guised mockery.

"I don't know. Would you like me to go up and
ask?" I gave it back.

"No, Mr. Know-all!"

"He cussed her a lot."

"Oh, your fabrications have no parallel," sighed
Sheila into the carrots.

I stepped into the dark of Madhu's cloister. The smell of incense hung in the living room. A table lamp glowed from under a black shirt thrown over it. The walls were covered with posters of gods and Indian movie stars. Next to the lamp, on the two-seater sofa, a lady's handbag lay half aslant. On the glass-top coffee table, there sat a lipstick and a broken glass bangle. Underneath, two pairs of sandals, one a man's with its bold leather straps, the other narrow and heeled, with elegantly painted silver designs from the Ajanta frescoes. The sandals were left close to each other, as if their occupants were holding hands, cuddling, before they eased themselves out and disappeared.

"She's in the bedroom," Madhu said, pointing the way.

"You lead," I said, eyes glued to the scissors in his hand.

He did. The bedroom was even darker. A tapered red candle burned on a plastic side table. The single bed was covered with a mosquito curtain that smelled of mildew and sweat. It hung from the ceiling by a large iron hook that had cracked the plaster into deep fissures. The ends of the curtain were tightly tucked around the bed. Someone lay motionless inside.

"Open the curtain," I said. My voice had lost its balance.

I couldn't see her face—the sari she wore was thrown over it to reveal the magenta velvet of her blouse with its reflective miniature mirrors sewn around the border. It had been ripped open. The tight white pants forced down to the ankles on which dangled ankle bells, the sort that nautch girls wear. Her stomach was bare except for where Madhu had repeatedly stabbed it with his scissors. I pulled the sari from her face. Madhu fell on his knees sobbing hysterically.

"I didn't meant to, I didn't meant to," he raved, banging his head on the bed frame with so much force that a bottle—until now hidden in the folds of the sari—rolled out on the floor. He went after it, trying to catch it before it broke. I grabbed his scissors and ran downstairs. It was only after I had locked my own door that I let out a roar. I was still buckling under when Sheila appeared.

"What's the matter?" she asked.

"Our friend upstairs committed murder!" I managed as I wiped my tears.

Sheila's mouth opened wide, then she quickly caught my look and waited for more.

"Our friend upstairs killed the redhead from the bazaar . . . I mean, he has killed her replica, a dummy . . . " I hadn't laughed this hard. "He has a dummy dressed up as an Indian."

"He has stabbed a doll?"

"Life-size, with tits, red wig, velvet blouse, underpants, everything under a stinking mosquito curtain with a rolling bottle of rum."

Sheila took a long minute.

"Poor man," she said.

I stopped laughing to look at her face. She was serious, even pensive. Didn't she understand what I was saying?

"What about the redhead he banged, then snipped into pieces?" I snapped as if in earnest, before my subdued mirth began to regather around my eyes.

"Poor man!" she said, and went to the bathroom.

Does laughter deepen one's compassion? Does it make the absurd in a sense serious and possible? Does it generate among those who have it pity . . . not the ordinary but the admirable kind, that grows into flowers, maybe? I fell silent and so did Sheila. It was as if I had so thoroughly exhausted the contents of a silly farce in advance that only silence could follow. We watched the TV, Sheila curled up on the sofa with her back toward me, a posture of self-absorption. I knew she was nibbling on her lip, trying to think of something to say if I broke the silence. I didn't want to. What I'd say might open a slow, reluctant row. Instead, I sat and let the TV drain me until the unreality of Madhu blended with the glitter parade of commercials singing of remedies to all human maladies. The more I watched, the more my mind wandered to the odd, contorted redhead upstairs with strips of hard cotton ripped from her belly, and Madhu, perhaps by now drunk and asleep beside her in the solitary glow of the red candle.

Madhu avoided me like an escaped criminal, shrinking from my presence in the hallway as if I were going to pounce on him. Alcohol had dripped into his sleeves and collars in dry, unmapped patches, and he stumbled out of sight or scurried upstairs to his sanctuary. In the dead of night, I heard him sob or move heavy things as if he were rearranging the disorder.

And one night I heard the old familiar voices return and once, a great cackle.

"Sears is getting rid of some mannequins," Sheila said one morning, her face flushed with excitement. I said nothing. She began trying the shirts she had bought. Sheila's breasts are small. They remind me of hyacinths heavy with dew. She stood in front of the bedroom mirror trying an orange shirt, her elbows raised, her head struggling to get in through the narrow opening, when I embraced her. The shirt was wet at the tails, for Sheila had laid it on the kitchen table to cut the tag; the wet ends grazed her nipples and her head, still above, her tousled hair glowing behind her like the strands of a silk lampshade. I kissed her breasts and gently held them in my palms. She went rigid for a moment, then she bent her head under the orange dome, surprised and pleased. We kissed, her thighs yielding to the pressure of my fingers as we reclined on the shag pile in front of the bedroom mirror. The only light in the room was the green arc on the stereo, evanescent and fulfilling, caught as we were in the irrevocable tapestry of seams and desires.

I neither saw the sewing box nor the bifocals, but a week later Sheila sat on the sofa with spools of colored threads and a needle between her teeth, scrutinizing irregular pieces of fabric.

"I've had these for years," she said.

"What are you sewing?" I asked, half apprehensive of the answer.

I had no desire for children. Even the thought of perpetuating my name was something that I didn't

45 GOSHEN COLLEGE LIBRARY
GOSHEN, INDIANA

believe in—to make a living, to be fully alive while writing, that was enough challenge. Sheila didn't like my attitude, but in her own way she drew similar conclusions; the hardships of rearing children in a city were crying out all around us. Then there were the fears parents lived with day-to-day—kidnapping, rape, murder.

"I'm making a new dress for . . . for Madhu's red-head."

"Oh. Since when have you become his seamstress?"

"Remember the day I told you about Sears?" Sheila ignored my rebuke. "Well, I talked to Madhu . . . he was so happy."

"Go on."

"There's nothing to go on! He asked me if I could fix up his torn one and I said yes. You should've seen the mess he made, trying to fix it himself!"

"Oh!"

"There's nothing wrong, is there?"

"What else did he ask you to do?"

Sheila threw her material down.

"I know what you're getting at! That's all you think. He was afraid even to sit on the same sofa. I brought the doll down to fix it."

I looked at the blouse she was making. Loops of thread hung around buttonholes yet to be tucked. Some were larger than others, and the hem of the burgundy piece still to be cut into the shape of the design on the paper appeared impossible. There were tiny buttons scattered over the sofa and around Sheila's legs. Her fingers were puffed and her eyes red.

"I'm sorry," I said.

"Okay. Don't make anything out of this. He respects us. He calls me his sister-in-law."

I kissed her on the neck.

"By the way," she added, wiping her tears, "Cindy is the redhead's name."

I imagined Madhu sitting in his room waiting for Sheila to breathe life into Cindy. His condition was hopeless. Sweat beaded permanently on his forehead. His clothes were the same as if they were now part of himself. His cowering in the hallway reminded me of the plight of the untouchables who inadvertently crossed the path of a Brahmin. Haunted men have bags under their eyes, but Madhu carried imprints of ancient coins. Sheila became the messenger between us. He felt terribly guilty about what he had made me witness that night. He slept with the fear I might turn him over to the police or to the asylum. He had nothing left in India. His parents were dead and his brothers and sisters had disowned him.

Are men born with accents as animals are with tails? In India, I worked for retired military officers who imitated the British so devoutly that they had taken over the habits and attitudes of their masters. One of them dressed in field uniform for breakfast, which was served by a turbaned servant in Victorian flourish: porridge, an egg cooked exactly three minutes and served in a silver egg cup with buttered toast, and orange marmalade. His wife kept the kitchen door shut so her husband wouldn't smell "the awful native stuff." Later in life, this man went so far as to speak with his family only if they made prior appointments. Whether such behavior extended to his love life was an unanswered question. Although he pretended to be British, he spoke like any other native planter, with one or two phrases coming off as if from the mouth of a character in a Raj movie.

Madhu held on to his thick Malayalam accent when he spoke English. When agitated, his speech came out in rapid fire. His "good mornings" turned into "goommorrney." Double s's, f's, e's and d's embellished his words, and the grammar of Malayalam fractured his English. When Sheila approached him about the mannequins, he became so turbulent that she couldn't figure out whether he was glad or upset. Despite all this, Sheila had a calming effect on Madhu. He stopped lining up garbage bags on the stairs and once or twice his shower shuddered into action.

"He has even swept the rooms, but he refuses to come downstairs," Sheila said after failing to persuade Madhu to join us for dinner.

Perhaps she pushed him too far, too soon. I began to notice her attempts seriously. She was keeping a madman alive, slowly turning his attention to functions of clean, proper domesticity. As if his impoverishment propelled her own hidden creativity, she experimented with Indian cuisine. She'd take leftovers upstairs and leave them at his door. Sometimes when he opened the door, I'd hear her caring voice. I'd sit tense, ready to leap over the steps if I heard her cry or shriek. Luckily, nothing untoward occurred, and when Sheila returned from her mercy missions, she glowed for the rest of the night.

I don't know when she finished stitching the burgundy blouse, but now she was making knickknacks. Several handkerchiefs, a scarf, napkins, and an Indian hat that looked very much like "You deserve a break today." *Would look odd on Madhu,* I thought.

Sheila's persistence must have worked, for Madhu appeared at our door on a Saturday morning dressed in a knitted shirt and baggy corduroy pants buckled tightly around his bean-stalk waist. The outfit was vaguely familiar. Madhu was scrubbed clean, but his hands kept fidgeting as if they were orphaned without something to hold.

"So sorree to bother," he apologized, taking a step backward. His bare feet left sweaty imprints on the threshold.

"Come on in," I said, opening the door.

"No no no. Why dirtee your house? Coming only to invite sissterr and self for tonight. Pleese come without fail." He bowed and left before Sheila joined me.

I congratulated Sheila.

"Should we?" I asked. It was my birthday and we already had plans.

"We must," she replied without hesitation, guiding my eye over to the stitched garments.

I helped her tie the box. It was full. This time we were both carrying it upstairs.

When we knocked promptly at seven, Madhu opened the door. He was wearing his old Nehru jacket, cleaned and pressed, with a pair of my old Levi's that had been stashed away for Goodwill. His suede shoes were also mine. I looked at Sheila. She winked. The living room was arranged differently. Heavy drapes were gone from the window; the sofa and the glass table had been moved to catch the diagonal light from the backyard. A soft, beige-colored spread was neatly tucked around the battered cushions of the sofa. Two large pillow-rests, still stiff in their newness, were propped on either side. The old posters were gone from the walls and the walls had been replastered and painted. An opaque divider curtain hung between the kitchen area and the living room. Shankar's double violin played distantly on a stereo. Madhu served drinks. I noticed his civility hadn't reached perfection, for he held the glasses with index fingers inside. Sheila disappeared behind the divider. I sensed her moving surreptitiously, arranging something. Madhu and I sat in silence, for without her I felt there wasn't much I could say. Madhu must've felt the same, for he reached nervously for a cigarette.

"Okay!" called Sheila, first peeking at us from behind the divider. Then she pulled it open. Five cane-bottom chairs formed a circle around a Formica table with a vase of dried wildflowers. Cindy sat in one of the chairs. She wore the burgundy blouse and the tight pants with her silver ankle bells. Her lips were stitched with new hard red threads, and she wore dark eyelashes that gave her a vacuous but hypnotic gaze. Several dazzling colored bangles adorned her wrists all the way up to the elbow. But for her red wig, she looked like a Rajput beauty.

"Let me introduce the others," Sheila said, standing beside the divider, pompous as a master of ceremonies.

"This here is Mr. Nair, Madhu's old roommate from Kerala. He may not look too much like the real thing, but this is what happens when Indians undergo cultural shock." She paused to look at me, giddy with her own humor.

"Next to Mr. Nair sits Mr. Menon, who aspires to be a lawyer. He likes to wear a dhoti and cross his legs in lotus fashion while drinking coffee."

Sheila made another pause to let me absorb the introductions.

"This fourth is Mr. Pai, now retired from civil service. He likes Western suits and ties."

Both Mr. Nair and Mr. Pai wore mine. Mr. Pai also wore the cap Sheila had made and held an unlit cigarette. Mr. Menon's bald plastic pate glistened.

"Do you like my friends?" Madhu suddenly asked, rubbing his hands, smiling like a schoolboy who had accomplished the impossible puzzle.

"I'm ssoo grateful to sissterr. My life is happee now!"

His sister took a bow and moved over to my side. I took a big gulp of the whiskey. Shankar in the bedroom hit a crescendo on the violin, and Madhu, as if on cue, went into the bedroom. When he returned, he held something that was covered by a large white kerchief. He handed it to me.

"I beg you do this one thing, pleese," he said.

It was a woman's wig with long black hair.

Sheila nudged. I walked over to the redhead and pulled out the wig. The black one transformed her completely. I took another gulp of my potion. There was something else I had to find out, something that had haunted me ever since the day Madhu had led me upstairs to the strange drama in his life. I put my drink down on the table, and with an abrupt move pulled down the dummy's pants until her belly was revealed. A pink scar, thinner than a strand of hair, ran across into her crotch.

"Thank yoo, thank yoo," Madhu was repeating with a bottle in hand.

"Let's go now," whispered Sheila, pulling on her gloves with the casual precision of a surgeon. I reached for her miraculous hand.

Immigrant Beginnings

Belur sat in the living room of his apartment, one leg tucked under the other in the posture of Lord Vishnu. But instead of holding a flower or mythic weapon in his hand like the deity, he held a mug of coffee that he blew on in sweet pleasure. At twenty-three, he was lean, healthy, and full of dreams. On streets among white Americans, his brown eyes and raven-black hair asserted a distinct identity. His easy smile and friendliness did not reveal a newcomer's solitude and uncertainty. Although he felt taller, his height hadn't changed in America. But his cheap mirror gave him that giddy illusion each morning.

Time had passed quickly since his arrival in Kansas. Only ten days ago, he had been hired as an assistant in Sporting Goods at King's Discount, America's most popular chain store (its catchy slogan was, 'King's Store is where your dollars score more.") Bob Buckskin, manager of Sporting Goods, led him to the aisle and briefed him on his duties.

"When you get here tomorrow, one of the girls will show you how to work the cash register. Today, I'd like you to change the tags on the fish hooks. There's a box of nylon jackets in the back room that should be put up for sale."

Brimming with fervor, Belur jumped to his duties. He quickly licked the little tags and tagged the fish hooks. Then he hung the made-in-Taiwan sports jackets in no time. As he moved from one task to another, he made little discoveries about his new position. Untagging and retagging were hard on jackets. The old price tags were pinned on top of coarse labels. He had to remove them before pinning on the new ones with other prices written below the printed ones. All $10.99's were now $9.69. What brought the sudden discount? he wondered. Maybe the owner made millions in Taiwanese stocks and passed on some reward to customers. Whatever it was, sticking a new label on the old with a bent pin wasn't easy. Over the intercom, salesmen announced price reductions with crackling frequency. It was like the closing night at a carnival. Buoyant branch assistants sang out their blue light specials, unadvertised specials, never-heard-of-such-a-thing specials. Salesgirls scurried through aisles of bargains playing hide-and-seek, while a calm voice from the courtesy desk repeatedly asked for this or that manager. The manager of Leather Goods was in an extreme hurry.

"These are going fast, ladies and gentlemen. A Lady from Big Bend, Wisconsin, bought a dozen belts. She says our prices upend King's at Big Bend."

Belur pinched himself, listening to the joyous market of voices. How lucky to begin a job with his own apartment in his new country. This king of King's Discount must be a benevolent millionaire. What a kingdom of discounts he possessed. Was his name really King?

The day went fast and as the clatter of feet and voices diminished, someone turned off the cluster of neon lights one by one. Bob Buckskin was counting receipts.

"Get rid of the empty boxes and go home. I'll see you Monday. By the way, you have a nickname?"

"No, sir."

"Forget the sir stuff. At King's, we're all equal. Velour, eh? It comes with you or is it extra? I'm kidding."

Belur grinned. These Americans made fun of everything. He placed the empty cartons in the crusher and walked to the front of the store. As he zigzagged through the aisles, a thin, tall man approached.

"Are you new here? You should walk straight through the main aisle when you're leaving." He pointed the way and stood there scowling. But for his manners and accent, he looked like another immigrant.

Belur apologized.

"Okay. Don't do it again," said the man, still scowling.

Bob Buckskin was handing over the day's money bag to a pretty young cashier, who blushed at something he said.

"Don got you, eh?" Buckskin said. "Don't worry. You'll get used to him."

The guard at the door made a mock gesture of holding open the door. "Good night, Sheikh!" he said. This was the Midwest, the heart of America, where making jokes was a way of life. But just to get even, Belur muttered quietly, "Good night, you mutton-head," and felt glad.

Already the streets were deserted. Here and there, a dog barked in someone's backyard, and streetlights rolled his shadow back and forth across the grass knolls that cupped the buildings. Cars lit up his face as they passed, as if scanning him for an identity. His tongue felt thick with the glue of hundreds of labels, and his thumb and index fingers burned from all the pinpricks.

"Hi. My name is Carla," the girl at the cash register said the next morning. She had auburn hair, which she wore up in a bun. Her lips were painted bright pink. Gold earrings and a stack of opalescent bracelets on her left arm jangled when she walked. Belur thought she looked like a movie star.

"Take a cart and pick up items from different departments and bring them back. I'll show you how to punch the register."

She turned away to attend to a customer. All the girls were totally absorbed, punching cash registers with calm, devotional efficiency. They wore blue jackets and the same golden earrings, but Carla's somehow stood out. Maybe it was her hair, or the bangles clinking as she moved back and forth on the register.

Were her lips pink naturally or juicy red? What a thrill to discover such a thing. Why did he like pink lips so much?

Belur wheeled the shopping cart into the aisle marked Electronics & Appliances. He was in a dilemma. What should he pick up? Carla had said something from every department. She should've said things that a poor shopper would pick up. A couple of customers with huge behinds blocked his way as they examined a washer-and-dryer set. Their young boy went around turning stereos to full blast. Nothing in the deafening E&A would fit into the cart. Belur decided to ask for help. He saw one of the pretty cashiers from the front desk sitting in the cafeteria with Don.

"Excuse me, but there's nothing in the E&A that'd fit inside this cart," Belur said to her. The girl smiled blankly. Don glared at him.

"Go get smaller stuff. Leave Electronics & Appliances alone," Don said with a smirk.

Belur pushed on to Housewares, embarrassed that he had run into Don, but proud that he had called Electronics & Appliances E&A, just like back home where abbreviating titles was a habit. He saw a beautiful red clock with black buttons. Next to it was a cheap imitation made especially for King's. "Compare the difference," the tag said. A whole three dollars less. He picked it up. The difference was obvious.

"Can I help you?" asked an old woman in King's blue who stood in the middle of the Kitchen section.

"I'm picking up things for register training," Belur explained. The woman stared for a second, then walked away. Huge varicose veins, blue as her King's coat, mapped the backs of her legs.

"How did you do?" Carla asked, smiling. She piled up everything next to the register. A silk negligée and brassiere from Lingerie were on top. "You went to town, didn't you?" She laughed. She must've liked his taste.

The negligée was red and the brassiere black. What color combinations did Carla wear, he wondered, while she showed him how to punch prices into the machine. Belur nodded, although he understood nothing. He undressed Carla and put on the black bra and the red negligée. Small beads of perspiration danced like pearls over Carla's pink upper lip. Perfume of some enchanting flower wrapped her body. Belur inched closer as her lips, absorbed as they were with figures, parted slightly.

"You see how it works?" Carla asked, ripping the receipt off the register and winking at him.

Belur forgot all about adding and punching. This was his first female wink in America. In India, women did not wink at men unless they were bent on mischief. Only whores winked freely. Good women probably winked in privacy, just as Carla was doing now. Here, winks were so spontaneous—he liked that.

"Take everything back. Bob wants you in Sports," Carla said, formal and businesslike. The brief dream was over.

"Sorry," mumbled Belur, looking around to make sure that no one had noticed the sudden awakening in his crotch. His attempts to calm it failed miserably. Belur pushed his body hard against the grill of the cart until his penis hurt. From a niche between Pots & Pans, the varicosed employee stared. When he was back in Sporting Goods tagging bats, balls, and batteries, his suspended erection wilted. But not before he had taken empty cartons to the crusher and pushed the button to watch the steel pistons extend and crush the waste into a wet lump.

Mrs. Morgan, the store manager, reminded him of the Russian Brezhnev. She sat behind a steel desk, her large nose and mole on the right cheek moving slowly to the words she uttered in a high dictatorial voice:

"Good Afternoon. I welcome you to King's Discount. You must always smile at customers. Always say 'Welcome to King's Discount, may I help you?' Payday is Thursday. No socializing between customers or opposite sex on duty. Wear plastic ID. Lunch break twenty-five minutes, dinner forty-five. No sitting while working . . ."

As Mrs. Brezhnev droned on, Belur wondered whether she, too, had varicose veins.

"Anything you wish to ask?" she asked after her speech and repeated the slogan, "Welcome to King's Discount" while grabbing his hand in an iron grip.

Belur thought she must have been a wrestler in her own country before she came to America. As he was leaving, Mrs. Brezhnev added one more thing. "You should always walk through the main aisle coming in or going out."

Belur reported back to Bob.

"Now you're in, all you need is a crew cut," Bob said smiling.

The first pay envelope came without any hitch. Mrs. Brezhnev marked his earnings and deductions right on top of the little brown packet. There was even a slot for coins. Everything was in order. In India, he would've had to wait in line to be paid, not to mention the many registers and clerks with ledgers waiting for his signature. Then there would have been servants and lesser clerks he'd have had to tip to keep them in good humor.

He went looking for Carla in the cafeteria. Sales-girls on break stretched their long, curvaceous thighs under the tables or up on empty chairs. Some unrolled their stockings to smooth their legs. In India, one never got a chance to see female legs so openly. Besides, under a sari, no amount of lifting legs would show anything. Traditional Indian women rarely shaved their legs. At King's, all the pretty young legs were shaved better than his chin! Carla wasn't there, but he knew her legs would out-match all.

When the older employees entered, the younger girls tried not to look at their legs. Deep blue veins, swollen like tributaries of wild rivers ran on the old legs. They were fat and hardly capable of being lifted. They were beyond repair. He heard the old ones talk of taking vacations, touring exotic countries like India to see the Taj Mahal in the moonlight, as if their fanciful longings could somehow anoint their ravaged legs. Belur remembered American tourists in India. Many of them looked like the old ladies of King's Discount. What good was it to wish for the exotic when the animal in one's legs had departed?

Carla's animal was very much alive and kicking.

—⬩—⬩—

Belur began his love letter this way:

> My beloved Carla,
>   Surely you must've been my wife in a previous life. How else would I be affected by your presence so quickly? I must've worshipped you like a saint or a mad lover for at least a century, sitting at your feet and looking up. When you smile, you're like the sun opening the lotus petals of my heart . . .

He read it again and again for mistakes. So far, it was touching but it needed words and meanings less Indian, for Carla might not know that lotus flowers opened only when the sun came out.

He went for an inspirational walk. What a thrill it was to walk on American streets! Everything clean and orderly—no milk cows jangling their bells, no milkmen yelling at them, no mongrels or donkeys peeing, no vendors, unruly crowds, no garbage dumps on side streets, no water puddles, no mosquito squadrons buzzing over one's head. He was dreamily lost when suddenly he heard a vehicle stop behind him. It was a police officer.

Belur immediately explained. "I'm a new resident in America. I'm taking a walk to enjoy the scenery."

"You're jaywalking. Don't they have traffic lights in India?" the officer asked.

"They're for cars," said Belur.

The officer smiled, nodding his head in disbelief. "I'll let you off this time. Don't do it again. Have a good day."

Belur jumped back on the sidewalk. Jaywalking! He didn't know the word, but it sounded great. Maybe the officer meant joywalking. In India, everybody joywalked everywhere and the police let them. Gandhi was always joywalking, and look what he had accomplished! Maybe he should end his letter to Carla with "I'll joyfully jaywalk to your heart."

At work the next day, Bob was particularly friendly, so Belur asked him about Carla.

"Why, you want a date with her?" asked Bob.

"No," lied Belur.

"Go talk to her. Tell her you like her tits," laughed Bob.

Belur hid his face among some coatracks. Soon enough at coffee break, Carla walked in wearing a transparent black dress; he could see her breasts thumping and jumping inside it. Oh, if he were only alone with her by an oasis with a jug of wine and Omar Khayyam!

"Hey Carla baby," yelled Bob. "Velour here has the hots for you."

Carla looked at Belur with a smile, crossing her legs and blowing rings with a cigarette. How carefree and wonderful! Belur could hardly keep his eyes steady. Love grew like a magical beanstalk inside him and invisibly he climbed it all the way to her proximity. A little voice whispered that he shouldn't wait too long to declare his passion. He waited until she finished the coffee and then cornered her in the aisles.

"Carla," he began, but his lips went dry.

"What?" Carla asked.

"I don't know how to say this," he stumbled.

"I'll make it easy for you. I get all I need from Don. Sorry," she said.

Belur was speechless. His heart burned, his face turned red and his temples bristled with pain. He felt cold and useless. Perhaps it showed on his face, for the guard came over to talk.

"Hey man, let me give you some advice. You just came to this country, right? Do good. Once you've got money, chicks come to you. All the owners of Wal-Mart, Woolworth's, King's, they didn't have no money. They came here with a few bucks and then they made it. Now they fuck everybody. Make money, Sheikh, you can buy all the ass you want."

Shocked and humiliated by the rude references, Belur felt totally lost. Everyone talked as if sex was the only thing that mattered. Even Carla had dismissed him by telling him about her affair. Was it an affair or was it forever? In America, men and women found sex before finding love, the exact opposite of his India. Strangely, Carla still held his heart in captivity. So what if she were living with that Sicilian Don, could he not rescue her with pure devotion? True love should overcome all problems. In Ramayana, Lord Rama's wife Sita was kidnapped by Ravana. When Ravana took her to his kingdom, she wouldn't let him near, so he left her in a sanctuary until she changed her mind. The epic said she never did, but didn't Lord Rama have doubts? He still rescued Sita.

Engulfed in such thoughts, Belur went to see Sidd, the owner of an Indian store who had given him shelter when he first came to this country. Sidd was prosperous and married to an Indian woman.

What Belur confessed didn't sit well with Sidd.

"You want to marry an American girl? They're sexy and striking, but it's all pomp and paint, lipstick and mascara. You marry one, for a few days it's all hunkydory, but then domestic life begins, it's all topsy-turvy. In married life it's the internal that counts, not the external. What about your parents? They sent you to make money and help them. Look at me, I skimped and saved and helped everybody. Now I can do whatever I want. Earn a living, make money, then when the time comes, find an Indian girl and marry."

Indian advice, American advice, it all sounds alike, thought Belur. He was hungry, both internally and externally. At Pizza Hut, he didn't have enough in his pockets to buy a whole pizza. As he ate a slice, a somber thought entered his mind: Carla drove a car, smoked expensive cigarettes, ate out, went to movies, not to mention other things she did with Don. Belur sent half his earnings to his parents, had borrowed money to pay the deposit on the apartment, and walked to King's. Most of the time, he existed on pizzas and grilled cheese sandwiches. He was a vegetarian. Could love instantly turn Carla into someone like him?

How could he bring his dreams into reality without money? No wonder all those immigrants before him, poor or poorer, also figured it out. Woolworth's, Wal-Mart, King of King's, all must've had love dilemmas, but they put first things first. Belur wandered listlessly. He wished to pee but restrained himself from doing it on a wall or a tree. In America, who knew where a policeman might be hiding? Maybe the policeman who once caught him joywalking was now watching his every move.

Not to test him but rather as if to confuse him further, many Carlas were driving cars, stepping out of doors, coming in or going out of buildings. Observed closely, they had different faces, some even prettier than hers and some with long dark hair like Indian women. America was full of beautiful Carlas who went by other names. Many were still growing, and in five or ten years they'd become full-blown Carlas. Belur felt a strange relief. Why should he hasten into situations? As long as one kept oneself healthy, good-looking, and prosperous, love could be found. Belur saw a middle-aged man encircle the waist of a very young, red-bloused Carla and walk her to his car. The man pressed her against the car door and kissed her. She kissed him back. No one cared. In fact, people walked by smiling. Belur imagined himself doing it. It was nice and American. He imagined kissing her against his own car. That was even nicer.

He went to bed with three things to decide: marriage, freedom, and money. Money came first, but knowing that, he dwelt on the matter of romance. For half an hour, he debated which came first in marriage—love before or love after? Both had possibilities, although he preferred the latter. He imagined a super-Carla waiting to wink at him at an appropriate time. He'd instantly marry her. If she had an affair, he'd tell her to get rid of it, like any other loving American. By then, he'd surely be American.

For the next half hour, Belur debated identity. He was Indian but slowly changing. He'd make rapid progress from being too much of an Indian to being not so much of an Indian. Changing external appearance wasn't a bad idea: crew cut, Levi's, sneakers, chewing gum—preferably Big Red. Why not? To be free, one must be fearless in the face of change. Day by day his fearlessness would grow in degrees. He'd be completely fearless by the time he was a citizen.

Then for the next whole hour, Belur tossed and turned. Money, money, more money. He wanted to rapidly move up the ladder at King's, then become a partner by tricks learned in the trade. For this, hard work and diligence were necessary. And a powerful motive. Hard work and diligence he had. Motive he would find. Belur felt the pinholes on his fingers from the tagging. He ran a finger over all the hurt fingers. I'll make a million for every hurt, he thought. He counted them. *One million, two million, three million, four, five, six, seven, eight, nine, ten, ten and a half, eleven and a half, twelve and a half.* He fell asleep.

Extraneous Details

I left the country. Once on TV, I heard G. Gordon Liddy say, "You can kill a man with a pencil." In the days when Mysore had a real king, a factory in the Bahusar Buildings made sandalwood pencils for the royal family. They were fragrant, almost balmy to the nose, but you couldn't chew them.

I steal pencils. Look up *pencil*: A little tail, diminutive of penis. An artist's brush. His individual skill or style. A cosmetic roll or stick for local applications. An aggregate of rays of light or other radiation, especially when diverging from or converging to a point. A one-parameter family.

Pencils were these things for me, before Liddy, before I gave in to the dark recesses in the soul of things, into the emptiness of beings—frogs, cats, dogs, boys, their hearts on a point. After that, pencils were easy to chew . . . the wood, I mean. The smell of felled trees was forever in my mouth. I dreamt of sprouting leaves from my hand and flowers from my hair. An expert in innocence, I achieved perfection before puberty. What few mistakes I made disappeared in the vanishing sameness that a pencil or pin understands.

What happened to the one I cared for isn't anyone's business. I wasn't strong enough to save the woman who could have been my wife. Like a pencil, I hid my sorrow at the blunt edge and I left. She was reborn as Reka the movie star on my video screen. I did what she asked. They were simple acts to accomplish. But when she wouldn't ask for anything, I practiced my art. One day, I would get even without her knowledge. I was glad I couldn't save her. Otherwise, what would have happened to my twin edges? A pencil has twin edges. "You need only one if you're smart," the schoolteacher used to say. I understood more than he thought. He had no imagination. But that was before I discovered pins. With a pin, everything is open. I moved to pins, between four to six inches, tensile, point or no point.

In biology, I pinned cockroaches in a dish, opened up their entrails to the clarity of water. Tiny separation of bloodless parts. Even cockroaches on their backs looked astonished at themselves, like multi-limbed gods. Seen movies where Romans crucified Christians. In one, the camera caught pins of light as it hit the nails and shone.

In America, I had to keep in shape, so I worked when I could. It was easy. I was ready when the message came from home, I said yes, for the sake of her, whose whereabouts were unknown. Three years, maybe five, but everything clear in my head—streets, trees, rivers, faces, her under him. No need for maps or languages. I was in.

The place, a dark plantation town. Time, evening. As I walked in, grains of sodden dust crept between my sandaled toes like miniature crabs. A vendor at the gate yelled.

"Sari for you, tourist Sahib? Gold and silver threads twining in Kamasutra. You Indian, no? Beautiful. Pfeel, pfeel."

He thrust the fabric to my face. The air smelled of wet jute, cow dung, animal sweat.

"I don't wear saris." I threw it back to him. Shadows in the archway stretched long in the simmering heat like in the de Chirico print on my wall.

"Hokay, hokay. How much you give me? You Kristani or Hindoo. Chalook to ho!"

A group of villagers buying something from a shop turned to look at me. The vendor grinned, his face now close to mine, mouth smelling of Arak. I pushed the vendor to the brick wall. Something hidden under his waist scraped the bricks.

"Pfuck you! Come back this way, you meet your pfate in my hand," he cursed.

The door was the fifth. I pushed it open easily. A narrow alley led to the inside. Smell of clay and liquor in the still air. Somewhere in the interior recesses, the tinkle of ankle bells. Silver and gold. Diamonds and rubies. Reka. Toenails painted in magenta. Feet arched like wings. Softness. Attar. A red muslin sari skirt with golden rose buds. Nothing underneath.

Reka walking away from my eyes. That sidelong glance with the pickerel smile. Then the quick eruption of her limbs like petals. In *Suhaag*, when Reka sings, ancient custom of our forefathers requires that the audience control their lust. So the clients in the dance hall hide their lust under cushions.

His name is Mulla. Profession, once a comic actor, now my contract. Last sighting over Reka. Fails to recognize me. Speaks of comedians.

"One Indian customer calling himself Charlee in one movie very pfunny. He play foreign returned Indian speaking only English. One day everybody out of the house and Charlee all by hisself with illiterate peon. Charlee say, 'Hey, peon, bring watter.' Peon misunderstanding accent, say, 'You want bottel, Sahib. I bring.' Hehchehee. Charlee pissed off. Next shot. Charlee calling peon. 'You pfool.' Peon saying, 'You want phool, Sahib. I bring.' He bringing one flower. Phool for Pfool, understand, hehehehee. Charlee choking and gasping, falling on floor. Very pfunny, seen thirty times crying like a baby with laugh. Only later moral of the story hitting the head. 'Charlee. Don't forget native things going abroad or you die.' Hehehehee. Charlee's wife good in bed, get it!"

TV is on. No ceiling fan in this dungeon.

"You have lice in your head," I say.

Mulla scratches his head. Sweat sprinkles off his hand.

"Once in a dream, my head was full of lice," I say. "I was looking for God and he was looking for me. I walked through a long corridor, scratching my head.

Lice fell in great numbers, some hurt and bleeding, some writhing in agony by the stabbing of my nails. Was my head being drained of unworthy parasites? All the fallen lice swelled with my brain blood and scurried away, fat as bed bugs."

"I see no lice in my head. I don't understand," Mulla said. Sweat poured from his face.

"Why did you set me up with the vendor?"

"The Sariwallah? I don't know him. Who are you? You're no tourist!"

I moved closer.

"Remember Reka?"

"The movie star? Who doesn't?" he relaxed a bit.

"No, somebody else, somebody you took."

"But that, that hasn't . . . you're here, for the money, right? They sent you?"

"I want that vendor's sari," I said.

"I have replicas. Here, take what you want." Mulla kept looking at my waist for a gun.

"No replicas."

"I'll help you. Take everything. They sent you, didn't they? They cheated me. I have more to give you. Opium from Lucknow. No, theirs. They cheat. I have Reka, too, here, my wife. You can have her. Pleese don't do anything."

The note in my pocket—*Your reward. Destination 200 miles from Kota Durga. Take bus. No baggage. Will be met. 5th door from the archway. No mercy.*

The vendor came, sat next to me. I gave him the note. He read, threw the sari on the bar. "Yours," he said.

"Salaam."

I threw the sari to Mulla.

"Wear it," I said. Did he know now?

"Wife not here," he said.

"Wear it now, strip and wear it, nothing else, now!"

The vendor said, "Yes, Mulla, wear it. It rains outside. I'll be in it like lightning in a cloud. Be quick."

"I never did anything," Mulla whimpered as he dropped his clothes and wound the sari around his buttocks. "I was pfoolish to take here and there. Everything now in this valise." He produced it, half dragging his nude body across the bar. "Leave me here and I'll never come back."

"Not the money. How's your deceit doing?" I asked as I slowly pulled the pin from my lapel.

Deceit—dhoka. I always liked saying it to perpetrators. I made a point of it—"A deceives B, B deceives C, C comes to you and says D, it's your turn. What then? It's complicated, I'm no deceiver. I like to stop it quickly. That's why I'm here."

"I don't understand," he trembled.

"Where's Reka?"

"Dead," Mulla said, and picked up a video. It was of the movie *Suhaag*.

"Play it," I said.

Mulla switched the VCR on and slid the movie in. He was recovering but unsure of what I was going to do to him in the sari. Underneath, his penis was half erect with fear.

I waited until the video Reka began the dance while Amitab drank. Then the rapists entered. Mulla stood on the side, casting his own presence on the video screen.

"On your knees," I said, and pushed him. The needle was swift and firm like my fingers. Mulla gasped and his mouth curved to hiss but lost the sound as he saw the light. I was wondering: *Was deceit already at the letter M?* It was good to stop it.

The sari was unblemished. I pulled it off of his body and carefully folded it. Did he recognize me? The needle went back into my lapel. Reka and Amitab had danced after getting rid of the rapists.

I left the valise, but shook a wad of bills over the sari. I walked through the archways onto the main road. Why did the vendor put on such an histrionic charade? Why didn't he do it? Not good or relevant questions. Curbing curiosity is a good habit. Details shouldn't jell into meanings. Talk can betray thought. Did I tell you of my other nightmare in which bathroom toilets always flood at my feet? I know what it means. Why should I give you details when they hold me in their sway? I show, I never tell. They wanted me, I wanted him.

A car was there near the deserted bus shelter. On the passenger seat, my breakfast wrapped in banana leaf stitched into a pocket with thin broomsticks. Next to it, the sari. I tore at the pocket, marveling how well it held. What fell out was a heart. Many mongrels roamed by the roadside cemeteries of villagers. I gave it to one with the eyes of Reka.

I'm back.

2

THERE

NOTE: All the stories in this section are set in a small town named Nanjangud in the State of Karnataka, in the south of India (known as the State of Mysore before the Indian Independence from British rule in 1947). Karnataka, along with the states of Tamilnad, Kerala, and Andra Pradesh, form the southern region of India. Heavily influenced by the British civil system and the English language, the southern states have steadfastly kept their mother tongues intact. Each of these states has a distinctly different language, and customs and superstitions peculiar to its various indigenous castes and tribes. But they all share certain characteristics and beliefs: the predominant religion is Hinduism, and society is agrarian, with many ancestral villages, temples, and forests. The weather is tropical, with a rainy season during July–September (also known as the monsoon season). With the exception of Kerala State, the level of rural literacy is low. Trusting their age-old ways and religious superstitions, villagers and townsmen live unperturbed by changes taking place in the bigger cities. Although these stories take place during the 1950s and 1960s, the characters are representative of the timeless beliefs and customs that prevail in the hearts and minds of most traditional Indians, regardless of where on the Indian subcontinent they were born.

Demon

After eight months of nibbling like sparrows on what they had saved in Mysore, Linga found a job as gravel carrier at a construction site on the outskirts of town. The hawaldar who controlled the gates opened them only when the siren came on. Once inside, Linga joined the long line of carriers to await his turn to be called. The hawaldar inspected each person's wrist for the blue indelible mark that identified them as approved workers.

"Sometimes there'll be some infection, but it'll clear up in five days," said the male nurse at the clinic who was in charge of marking Linga on the first day.

But the wound spread under the skin into the shape of a small flower like the wild blue iris that grew in the millet fields of Nanjangud, his hometown. Linga was proud of this tattooed flower. The hurt wrist was the badge of his wage-earning identity. He was no longer a starved face at the gate of factories, shoving and pushing other faces for any available chance at a day's wage.

Linga often pinched his wound to remind himself of his good fortune. When he did, pus cleared from the outer edge of the healing scars and blood spurted in dots on his skin. His wife Shanti covered her eyes at this self-torture.

Linga would tease her. "If you stayed in Nanjangud, you'd have gladly given your arm to be tattooed for the sake of fashion. Now you turn your face away from my blue flower!"

They had left Nanjangud soon after the wedding, when the mango orchard Linga had cultivated withered under two long years of drought. There were no jobs with the only grain merchant in town. When they went to the city of Mysore, all the big grain merchants hired families of farmers. Jobs passed on from father to son, uncle to nephew, brother to brother. Competition was fierce. One merchant was willing to give Linga a chance if he left Shanti behind. But Linga and Shanti would rather have pawned their valuables or starved. One day, beating others to an opportunity at the railway station, Linga carried the bulging suitcase of a stranger who turned out to be the new manager at the factory.

Nine days after Linga was employed, the hawaldar joked at the gate about his flower.

"You keep squeezing it and soon it'll send roots up your ass!"

Even now, this was not the way Linga and Shanti wished to live.

"What's the use of living like slaves chained to this factory? Once construction is finished, they'll throw us back on the streets," Shanti would say in bed.

"I know. But if we go back, we need money to buy new saplings," he would remind her.

Construction on the first floor of the factory was going well. The manager respected the wishes of workers and offered huge squashes smeared with red kumkum to the evil spirit that controlled the safety of the construction. Mock human faces drawn on the squashes were smashed at appropriate spots. The kumkum mixed with the flowing juices of the squashes and ran like blood. This was the way to fool the evil spirit into thinking that real blood had been shed to appease its anger. Once the first floor was finished, work began on the stairway to the second, where cracks suddenly developed. The stairway wobbled dangerously as the coolies walked.

"It's the demon spirit!" declared the foreman who supervised Linga's gang. "I've seen this happening at other sites. When you construct a building with more than one floor, you must offer sacrifices at every level."

Linga knew of a similar incident involving a bridge that was built over the Kabini River in Nanjangud. The British engineer scoffed at the laborers who had asked that a rooster be offered to the bridge. When construction was over, the skeptical engineer triumphantly drove his car across it, only to miss the last span and swerve into the river. It took the temple elephant two hours to pull out the crushed automobile. The engineer was a good swimmer, but his dog drowned. A few months later, the engineer caught a strange disease that made him roll his tongue uncontrollably and spit blood. He died soon after.

Even the hawaldar was concerned. "This demon must be a city demon. I don't think it can be fooled with squashes. The management is talking with the priest," he said.

Linga informed Shanti of all the happenings.

"Don't involve yourself with anything that might anger the spirits," she warned him. Shanti was afraid. She was getting sick regularly in the mornings. A pregnant woman, she knew, was prone to attract evil spirits. Stories of demons entering the fetuses of unborn children were common. She vowed that she'd sacrifice a hen to Goddess Kali at the temple if everything went well.

The next Monday at the factory, a goat's severed head hanging over the stairway relieved the coolies, who worked at a greater pace. It was best to finish the stairs before the appeased spirit changed its mind. Linga was in the forefront, working harder than any other, urging everyone to speed up. The second floor was completed without incident. Linga was given a bonus.

"If the factory is completed before the deadline, we can go back to Nanjangud for the birth of the baby," he told Shanti.

But the third floor was a disaster. Slabs of half-dry cement fell with uncanny aim on the heads of coolies. The hands of masons were caught under bricks, and even veterans were cutting or bruising themselves. The first aid clinic was running out of bandages.

The foremen assembled everyone. "This demon is smart. It waits for a sacrifice to be made, then it doubles its demands. I've also heard they change shapes."

"We should hire it to bargain for us," joked one worker.

"Even our fearless hawaldar is now scared. He asks Linga to run his errands."

"Linga is the only one who isn't injured by anything. Maybe we ought to offer him to the demon next!"

Although Linga was untouched by accidents, he was having strange nightmares. In one, a beautiful woman kept making advances, but just when he was about to be seduced, she took her head off. Linga woke up screaming, for he didn't wish to see the rest. But each recurring nightmare took him closer, and in the last one he saw dark pores around the apparition's neck.

"I've been having strange dreams, too," confided Shanti, but she did not tell him what they were. She was now big, and Linga couldn't hold her without feeling clumsy and passionless.

Construction on the third floor halted for the arrival of a famous sorcerer. Linga was put in charge of supervising masonry work on the second. Several coolies were laid off as work slowed. When the sorcerer arrived, he at once began rituals, some of which were done after-hours in private. Only the hawaldar knew of them.

"The sorcerer is worried because the demon is resisting," he told the rest of the crew one day.

Linga secretly relished his new position on the second floor, especially since he supervised women coolies, who carried paint and plaster materials. Shanti had no interest in sex, and the women coolies were young. They liked his teasing. One or two seemed willing to go further.

"I've noticed your romancing," said the hawaldar. "But don't get me wrong. I know how it is when there are problems at home and temptations at work." The hawaldar could pick and choose the women coolies. Those that obliged stayed working.

One afternoon the hawaldar asked Linga to the first aid clinic.

"They wish to check your blue flower. It seems some of the ink they used was contaminated," he said.

Linga's flower was healed, though the edges were still pink. He scratched to make sure no pus came out. At the clinic, a young woman doctor/nurse he'd never seen before was peering into a microscope.

"Shut the door," she ordered him.

Linga obeyed. There was something in her voice that sounded familiar. He waited for her to turn from the microscope. She had tied her long black hair in blue ribbons and let it hang over her white doctor's coat. She was tall. She wore large, disc-shaped earrings made of buffalo horns.

"Take your clothes off and sit on the table," she said as she turned to look at him. Linga couldn't believe what he saw. It was the woman from his nightmares. He quickly glanced at her neck.

"Do not be shy. I see bodies every day." She advanced toward him. There were no pockmarks or pores on her neck. It was graceful as a peacock's. Linga turned his back and undressed, for he didn't wish her to see his face. She giggled when he stripped to his underwear.

"What a beautiful flower." She touched his scratched skin and looked at him inquiringly.

"I scratched it to see if there was any pus," Linga explained.

"This isn't an iris but a mango bud about to blossom." She was oblivious to him.

"Maybe it is to a doctor with microscopic eyes," he taunted.

She moved closer and began touching him, running her hands over his chest, then over his lips. She held his chin.

"Kiss me!" she ordered.

Instinctively, Linga looked at the door. The perfume on her earlobes was overpowering. Linga felt the surge in his loins. He pulled her head down and began to kiss her.

"No, no, no. Not this way." She suddenly freed herself. Her sari fell from her shoulders. Someone knocked. It was the hawaldar.

Linga was hauled in front of the owner, Mr. Achar. He was trembling, expecting to be fired for misbehavior. It was not his fault. The woman had led him on. But who would listen to the truth in matters of sex? Such a beautiful woman must have many admirers in the factory, but she had chosen him!

"We're most concerned about the demon," began Mr. Achar instead. Linga sighed in relief. "Everyone says you're the one it hasn't hurt for some lucky reason. You must help us." Mr. Achar held a wad of new rupees for Linga to help himself to. The hawaldar made signs with his eyes for Linga to go ahead. Linga took the rupees.

Outside again, Linga tried to talk to the hawaldar, who wasn't interested in hearing what had happened in the clinic.

"Before you appeared, Achar Sahib told the manager to appoint you as foreman. This is your lucky day, and you're now one of us. The manager is throwing a party tonight for you. I'm to escort you." The hawaldar clicked his heels in a military manner, mocking Linga's changed status.

Shanti listened in a stupor, for she had been put on drugs to kill the agonizing cramps that seized her frequently. Her belly was astonishingly large, as if she was carrying more than one child. Linga was thankful that her condition made other matters easy to ignore. He didn't have to explain about his encounter at the clinic.

When he reached the manager's bungalow that night, a large table in the living room had been covered with a festive cloth, as if for a dignitary. All the windows had been shut from the inside and the manager's family was away.

"Welcome, welcome," greeted the manager, embracing him. The hawaldar, who was opening a bottle of whiskey, and the foreman who supervised construction on the first two floors were the only other guests. Linga drank the whiskey in quick toasts. He was no coward. While they sat drinking, Naidu of the Biryani Hotel appeared with trays of food. The manager addressed him with jocundity.

"Hey, Naidu. Achar Sahib made Linga a senior foreman. Watch how you talk to him!"

"I know Linga is a hardworking man. It's only fitting that he got rank now," said Naidu, suddenly obeisant and pleading as his eyes danced around the open whiskey bottle.

Linga poured some whiskey into a glass.

"Here, Naidu. This is the real stuff, not the rotgut, black market poison you're used to. Thank your stars."

They laughed, and Linga was immensely happy. While they ate the many things Naidu had brought, their lusty drinking emptied several bottles, which piled up against the wall. Linga had dreamed of this life of class all his life. Now it burst upon him with sudden excess. But what he had to do for the factory wasn't clear. Everyone thought he possessed some strange power or alliance with the demon, while in truth he was as puzzled by recent events as anyone else. Those nightmares and the shock of the doctor/nurse's strange behavior would not normally have turned his life topsy-turvy, yet here he was amidst giddy abundance. Perhaps he could think of something to do to make the demon go away. There must be some trick. It would occur to him. Wasn't he the quick-witted charmer of women coolies? Wasn't he the one who goaded them to work faster than the demon's changing mind?

A hand gently shook him from his reveries. He was shocked to see it was the doctor/nurse's. Linga quickly looked for his comrades, who had vanished.

"I want you to know that I didn't betray you. I will prove it. Take me," she said, falling on her knees and kissing his tattooed iris. She licked it, sending ripples of pleasure through his body. There was an overpowering smell of ripe mangoes about her, as if she had rolled in a field of golden fruits.

Linga thought of the old orchard where he had ripened mangoes in folds of hay, hiding them from the monkeys and crows. The doctor/nurse was kissing his waist now. She ripped open his shirt and pulled him down onto the floor. When her lips covered his mouth, Linga, inebriated, lost consciousness.

His new friends were back when the hawaldar shook him, slouched on the chairs in drunken indifference to what had occurred. *Surely they must've seen her*, Linga thought, but there was no trace of the doctor/nurse and no one listened to his babblings.

"You fell and hit your head hard on the floor," said the hawaldar. "For a first-time party drinker, you're pretty good." Nothing else mattered, or so it seemed.

After a while, the manager addressed him with unexpected formality.

"We know the only way we can proceed with the third floor is to give the demon what it wants. The sorcerer says it'll only reveal what it desires to a pregnant woman."

"What should I do?" Linga asked without thinking.

"Take your wife to the factory at dawn this Saturday. She must perform a puja on the third floor."

When Linga explained all this to Shanti later that night, her pains and her superstitions began to grow. What if the displeased demon turned its wrath against her? Already, she felt the baby convulsing with inexplicable agony.

On Saturday, a tonga sent from the manager took them to the factory. The hawaldar and manager Narayan handed her baskets of fruit and wildflowers.

"Our sorcerer predicts good things for you and the factory. Go to the third floor and offer puja to the demon. When this is all settled, you and Linga can live free for the rest of your lives in the living quarters we plan to build next."

The hawaldar escorted them to the stairway and opened the door, which had remained shut since the accidents. Linga caught his wink and quickly led Shanti up the dark flight of stairs. What did the hawaldar wink for? Linga took it as encouragement to get it all over quickly. Or did it mean that the hawaldar promised other things, like the doctor/nurse? Why was Linga asked to leave Shanti alone on the third floor and to wait on the second until she finished the puja?

Linga loved Shanti, but ever since the doctor/nurse had accosted him at the clinic, he couldn't think of anyone but her. If he felt a misgiving as to what might happen to Shanti, he kept it to himself. He was no longer a simple farmer. A hunger within now asked for power, attention, and impossible love. What had happened at the party? Had he made love with the doctor/nurse? He must have, for he could still smell mangoes on his skin.

The half-finished third floor was dark. The only completed window was now boarded from the outside.

Unopened sacks of cement lined the wall in a semi-circle and a red ribbon was pinned on one. Shanti calmly went about preparing the clear space in front of the sacks. She dusted a small area with her sari and began placing the ingredients for puja. She was in a world of her own, and Linga retreated cautiously. When he reached the stairway, a voice asked him to stop. It came from behind the cement sacks.

"Who is there?" he asked.

There was no answer. Linga walked back to where Shanti was arranging the flowers and saw that she had fainted, her head propped on a cement sack, her enormous belly wobbling as if the baby inside kicked in some urgency.

"Here!" said the voice, now close. The lighted incense sticks formed rings in front of Linga's face.

"You're a foolish man. I warned you in your dreams. You should've left when I warned you!" The bodiless voice moved closer. Linga fell to his knees.

"Look at me," the voice commanded, and Linga fearfully obeyed. It was the doctor/nurse, but she was not human. Her expressionless face was a mask concealing another unthinkable one, a hideous terror only felt in nightmares.

She untied her hair, sat next to Shanti's prostrate body, and began to sway her head over the protruding belly. Closer and closer she moved, and the baby inside convulsed with panic. When her face was almost on Shanti's stomach, the demon seemed to stick her tongue out to lick. Shanti began to moan, and the demon joined in. It was impossible to separate the two for a while. The wails fought each other in unison until Shanti's voice gained an incandescence, as if it were turning into a prayer, an incantation. Linga heard notes that were seeking help in the tremulous wail. Suddenly, the moaning stopped and the demon rose, holding the wild bunch of iris Shanti had clutched in her hand.

"Take your wife and go back to your village. I'm tired of eating flesh. I'm tired of crafty men," the demon said, her face grown softer, still unsteady, indecisive.

Linga grabbed Shanti and dragged her away from the demon. When he reached the stairway, the demon was gone. Linga couldn't remember how he managed to climb down with Shanti. There was a storm brewing in the afternoon sky. Lightning etched angry branches over his head. As they left the factory, Linga thought he saw the demon walking swiftly toward manager Narayan's office. If Linga heard a scream, perhaps it was only his imagination. He thought more about the rain that now poured over their submissive heads. His orchard would be full. He looked at Shanti's belly, wet through the sari, wobbling as if in relief. There would be mangoes in the orchard when they returned to Nanjangud.

Iyer's Hotel

There was one place in Nanjangud where the meals were always good and where every eccentric who came to eat paraded his oddity without the least bit of embarrassment—Iyer's Hotel. In the days of the British, it had been called Iyer's Vegetarian Pub, after its founder, Rama Iyer, who had built separate areas for foreigners, local families, and a backdoor room for the lower-class customers who ate from discarded aluminum plates that had survived the first two classes. After Rama Iyer passed on, his eldest son leveled the compartments and created a single hall like that of any other Hindu hotel.

When the British left, the surreptitious serving of liquor from Rama Iyer's private stock in porcelain teacups ended, and the hotel became a true vegetarian place. An upstairs hall was built to house the Brahmin cook and servers. The urchins who washed the dishes slept on the back veranda, where sacks of flour, vegetables, rice, and condiments were kept. Abba Seth, the Persian cat belonging to the Iyer family and now too old to play, had his own special pile of empty sacks to reign from. The foraging rats had discovered Abba Seth's infirmity and now ran around fearlessly. Abba Seth looked on, dreaming of his youth. But even in his youth, being an aristocrat, he had had alley cats to run his errands.

Mani Iyer, grandson of Rama Iyer, was now in charge of Iyer's Hotel. He didn't pay much attention to the physical condition of the place, and the marble tabletops his grandfather had imported from Sorrento had long cracks where small insects lived, oblivious to the plates and tumblers that constantly banged on their roof. The once-whitewashed walls were dirty, and some of the nail holes were covered by three huge portraits. In the eastern corner, Lord Shiva stood with his right foot poised threateningly over the universe; over the entrance to the kitchen, Lord Krishna, in one of his many forms, hugged milkmaids; behind the cash desk where Mani Iyer sat, Goddess Lakshmi stood on an open lotus and smiled benignly at Mani Iyer's widening patch of baldness. The chairs wobbled and some had lost their arms. A large ceiling fan creaked laboriously until it reached its one speed. A sign encircled with bulbs announced the hotel in both English and Kannada, and in the evenings, while the gardener watered the flowerpots on the front steps, Mani Iyer turned up the radio and switched on the colored lights.

On Saturday morning the usual assortment of townsmen gathered at Iyer's Hotel. Javare Gowd, popularly known as Comrade Cumin, was the first to arrive. He was a man of means, having inherited land that he leased to farmers, reserving one acre on which he cultivated herbs. CC, as he was called, was a staunch supporter of a return to vegetarianism and the wonders of cumin. He kept a cumin plant in a brass vase on his table in the eastern corner. When the plant withered, he replaced it.

One of CC's pet topics was why India had deteriorated after the British left. "All the British did was teach us bad eating habits. Why, some of us even think it degrading to eat greens cooked with our own herbs, by our own women! Our irrigation minister has to have poached eggs and whiskey for lunch. Our leaders are corrupt and weak because they imitate British habits!"

If anyone disagreed, CC grew hysterical and pounded the table until the tumblers shook, his breath reeking of cumin. At least CC was right on one thing: It was better to have cumin on your breath than acid indigestion.

When Gem came around, even CC stopped his speeches to listen. An orphan brought up in the temple chowltry, Gem was the self-appointed, official tourist guide and agent for the area. He had an uncanny grasp of languages and spoke enough English to pass as a college graduate. He traveled between Nanjangud and Mysore City every day in search of tourists. He was also the town's middleman for villagers who came in with goods to sell. No villager could enter Nanjangud without Gem knowing about it, but he charged a smaller commission to the villagers than he collected from the merchants. This gave him a reputation as a man who cared.

With a Gold Flake in one hand and an unopened tin of cigarettes in the other, Gem would enter Iyer's Hotel and order coffee and the English newspaper that Iyer kept under his cash desk. He'd spread out the newspaper, place the ashtray in the middle, and start to read, shaking his head in disapproval. Many who came to Iyer's Hotel waited for Gem to keep them abreast of the news. Some would buy him breakfast, which he'd accept without displaying the slightest interest in it, but while eating he'd say something especially useful to his benefactor.

One day the talk was about the lightning storms that were passing through the country. Gem translated an article in which a famous guru claimed that God was upset about the erosion of faith in his favorite nation and was trying to warn its people. The senior constable, a devout Muslim, had barely escaped a thunderbolt while seeking shelter under a tree.

"God doesn't care if you're Hindu or Muslim, as long as you believe in him," said Gem.

Shetty, of Badami Store, the only store in town that stocked prayer books along with rare spices at black market prices, had read a book on Vedanta. "God doesn't arbitrate. He starts one action, then goes on to another one. He doesn't make a habit of checking up on his actions to see how they are doing!"

Shetty was sitting in front of the halva, tapping his spoon over the soft saffron glob and licking syrup from the bottom. Shetty would fondle the halva this way for a long time before eating it.

"God shows his displeasure to believers as well as nonbelievers," Shetty continued. "He can drop a tree on someone's head as well as beside it!" He looked triumphant and sliced his halva with a spoon. The server was waiting for him to order his masala dose, which he did after he chewed on the halva, making it obvious how good but expensive it was.

CC was still unconvinced. "Instead of taking chances, why doesn't God just yell at us, like everybody else does?" he wanted to know.

Before Shetty could think of one of his make-believe quotations from Vedanta, Gem snapped, "God used to do that, before he gave man a mouth!"

As though God wanted to score a point in favor of Gem, Shetty, who had finished his halva and opened up his masala dose at its fold to be sure that the cook had put plenty of butter on the fried potatoes, let out a cry. There was a dead lizard inside his dose. Mani Iyer came running from his desk. After he had made sure it was indeed a lizard and not a whole, hybrid red chili that had escaped the cook's knife, he picked up the plate and ran yelling into the kitchen. Within minutes, he returned with a brand new masala dose, twice the size of the first.

"It was just an accident, Shetty. Somehow a stray lizard climbed up on the wall beside the stove. It must have inhaled the pure fragrance of our recipe and fallen into the dose while the cook was folding it. I made this one myself. I've examined it thoroughly—it's ship-shape, and it's on the house."

Seeing the size of the dose and the way it still siz-
zled in its butter, Shetty calmed down. The others
sat in silence, staring at Shetty's dose and then at their
own empty plates. They wondered about comments
on Iyer's Hotel made by those who patronized others.
Until now, they had thought such comments were
simply clannish. True, the plates were greasy, cockroaches had nursed their young ones in the sweets,
and houseflies committed hara-kiri in the coffee
tumblers, only to surface with a vengeance at the
drinkers' lips.

By the time Shetty had become absorbed in the new
dose, there was another commotion. A rat dashed out
from the kitchen, followed by the cook. The rat was an
expert in skirmishes, and each time the cook cornered
it and raised his batter ladle, it slipped under a customer's leg. The customers cooperated by lifting their
legs and shouting suggestions, but the rat evaded the
cook's brandishing pursuit and, climbing into the glass
cabinet where sweets were kept, hopped into a large
bowl of jamoons. It swam in the syrupy bowl for a
while and finally climbed out, its eyes ecstatic and
glowing with sugar dust. Mani Iyer, who had joined
the chase, caught it with an expert pounce of his fist
and hurried into the kitchen with the cook. There was
much screaming and yelling.

Customers in the hall began to discuss the hotel's
sanitary conditions and wondered whether they had
already been contaminated. Some took the opportunity to slip out without paying. The regulars stayed on
for a while out of loyalty, then they too left.

Mani Iyer sat at his desk, occasionally hitting himself on the forehead in despair. The incidents of that
afternoon had grown into fabulous exaggerations as the
story spread. It was said that the hotel was not only
contaminated but haunted. On Friday nights ghosts of
the departed British sang and danced on the roof while
Mani Iyer's ancestor Rama Iyer, also a ghost, served
them liquor in coffee tumblers. Children were forbidden to urinate around the foundations because of a
strange smell that only religious women could discern.
Soon, business at Iyer's Hotel trickled to nothing. On
top of all of this, Abba Seth was discovered in the back
alley in the company of two muscular rats who were
rummaging through his body as if looking for something they had forgotten. Abba Seth was quite dead.

"God is chastising the Iyer dynasty for its miserli-
ness," declared Shetty, who now patronized a rival
hotel where credit was freely given.

Mani Iyer gathered his remaining friends over
breakfast. After CC failed to convince him that burning cumin in the hall might disinfect the premises, he
pleaded with Gem to think of something.

"Maybe I can, maybe I can't. I have no spare time,"
replied Gem.

"Take some time off from guiding tourists. I'll pay
you if you bring back my customers."

"People are saying your rats have bubonic plague.
Imagine working against that sort of mentality,"
replied Gem, tapping his Gold Flake thoughtfully.

"I'll pay 150 rupees for your services. It's more
than you make in a month. Here, take ten rupees in

advance." Mani Iyer pulled the note from his pocket and gave it to Gem. The note had turned wet.

Gem stared at the note as if he were insulted. "The best thing is for me to sit near the front door every morning eating my breakfast. People will see that nothing happens to me."

Iyer quickly wiped his face with his shoulder towel. He looked ten years older.

"This will ruin me, but I'll let you eat. Just don't ask any of your friends to sit with you," he replied wearily.

The best marble top in the hotel was pulled close to the front door, and Gem arranged his business cards and stationery on it. The server was instructed henceforth to keep the English newspaper on Gem's table, with a clean ashtray and hot coffee in the porcelain pot that Iyer kept for dignitaries.

If only his parents were alive, watching him with admiration as he sat every morning in Iyer's best chair, eating whatever he wanted and reading the English newspaper! He had heard that a woman who had drowned in the Kabini was his mother, but no one knew where she was from. When he had been found in a tomato basket on the steps of the temple chowltry, in a frayed undershirt with "G.E.M." embroidered on the neck, the trustees had surmised that he was a Brahmin orphan. He could never figure out how the red thread and initials had indicated his caste. Maybe it made matters easy, since the chowltry was only for Brahmins.

One morning as he sat at breakfast, Gem was shocked to read of antique hunters from foreign countries who were bribing innocent villagers to steal centuries-old statues from village shrines and ancient ruins. A Muslim mosque had recently been robbed of an illuminated manuscript, and the police had arrested some suspicious characters from the Tibetan settlement near Mysore City. Gem decided he should go there immediately and investigate.

"Keep thinking about my problem, not just tourist problems," said Mani Iyer.

A few days later, Gem returned in a state of rare excitement.

"We must perform a purification ceremony. We will move the glass cabinet where the rat caused the havoc and have our head priest purify the area. We'll announce the rituals in our newspaper so everyone will realize we are doing the right thing."

A reluctant Iyer went back to his cash desk to figure out expenses while Gem sought out the temple priest and the editor of the *Nanjangud Nutshell*. The priest readily agreed, but the editor haggled a bit over giving the top half of the front page to the hotel without at least a whole case of beer.

The glass cabinet was moved aside and the coolies began cracking the cement floor. Gem asked them to finish their work before dusk and to leave the pit untouched.

"Don't take offense. It's one thing for you to come and eat at Iyer's Hotel anytime you want, but when it comes to ceremonies, we have to have the Brahmins and the temple priest present. They won't do the spirituals unless we make them think the place is all theirs."

The workers laughed. They were always the ones to do the dirty work before the priest came and claimed everything was holy. They finished the digging, cleaned up the dirt, and left with their wages, which were extra-generous.

When Gem went to fetch Mani Iyer, he was full of cheer. He told Mani Iyer to lock up the hotel until the priest arrived for the morning ceremonies.

By eight the next morning, Mani Iyer had brought the necessary ingredients for worship. He had made a special trip to the Kabini River to bathe and pray. The priest chanted over the pit, which was covered with a sacred cloth, sprinkled holy water over each corner and implored whatever gods were angry to have mercy. By the time he lit the camphor and walked three final times around the pit, tinkling his silver bell, quite a few people had gathered. Finally, the priest lifted the cloth and asked everyone to throw flowers into the pit. Gem suddenly noticed something glimmering under the petals. With the priest's consent, he entered the pit and removed the shining object from the clay. "My God!" he exclaimed as he picked it up and held it so everyone could see.

In the bright of day, the object sparkled. When Gem slowly twisted and turned it in his hand, everyone gasped at the dazzle of the precious stones. Rays of blue, red, and green shot at them, making them blink. It was clear that the object was not a Hindu or Muslim relic.

"It's a holy icon of the Christians!" Gem said.

"Imagine finding a Christian object under a Hindu hotel!" mused CC when the excitement had subsided.

"A sacred object is sacred regardless of its origin," declared the priest, who was convinced that his chanting must have had something to do with the discovery.

Gem brought the icon to the cash desk and asked Mani Iyer to stand beside him for the cameraman. The cook reluctantly parted with the only good stool he had in the kitchen. The icon was placed on the stool between two incense sticks and some marigolds Iyer pulled from the flowerpots.

The news soon spread to the Anglo-Indian population living in the Railway Lines. The Methodist principal from the Mission School was the first to arrive with his family.

"This is the most glorious event in our lives," he said after a quick glance. His family knelt by Iyer's desk to say a prayer.

For once, the editor of the *Nanjangud Nutshell* was inspired. He wrote: "A mystery surrounds the discovery of a golden icon in the foundation of Mani Iyer's hotel. An area of the Hotel had been excavated to get rid of evil spirits that were polluting Iyer's food, and a golden icon believed to be hundreds of years old was discovered. The icon has been identified by the Mission School principal as Portuguese. Iyer's Hotel will remain open every day."

Iyer's Hotel became a pilgrimage center for believers as well as skeptics. Naturally, after seeing the icon, they ordered food and coffee so they could sit and gossip. Even womenfolk who never went to eat in a hotel came, using the occasion as an excuse to lunch out. After all, it was as special as going to worship, and who knew what blessings they might receive!

Iyer was beaming, but that didn't stop him from thinking of the future.

"Maybe my hotel sits on buried treasures belonging to my ancestors," he speculated, to make his claim clear.

"Your ancestors had nothing to do with Christianity except to entertain a few Englishmen. If there's any treasure, it belongs to the Hindu kings who owned all this territory, including the land your hotel sits on!" remarked CC.

Father Xavier of the Exiled Goans' Association of Bangalore was willing to buy the relic for his members. But, of course, Mani Iyer wouldn't part with his lucky charm.

Gem made repeated trips to the newspaper to make sure that it said something about Iyer's Hotel and how the icon united Nanjangud's religions under one roof, along with the specials of the day that the cook now prepared. He concocted a new appetizer called Icon Chowchow, and tourists were photographed standing by the icon and eating the chowchow. Iyer had to hire extra servers, the glass cabinet was back where it belonged, and no one asked what had happened to the proposed purification ceremonies.

In private, the editor of the *Nanjangud Nutshell* felt that the icon really did not belong where it was found.

"It looks too clean, too polished to have lain there in the earth below for who knows how long," he said.

"Editors like him are eccentric. Doubting is their professional hobby," Gem responded when the news reached him. "By doing so, they forget the consequences they create."

Iyer was adamant and so were his supporters.

"I'm a Brahmin, but miracles have no attachment to religion. They happen to Hindus, Christians, Muslims, and even atheists. The point is how they happen and what benefit such happening brings to us. Beyond that, only a fool would question their mystery," Iyer defended the discovery.

Everyone agreed.

Soon, the editor of the *Nanjangud Nutshell* gave up his detective speculation and Iyer treated him well, with discounts on what he ate. Gem kept hopping between Nanjangud and Mysore City, and sometimes he would return with things wrapped in a bundle under his shoulder.

Although the *Nanjangud Nutshell* did not print it, elsewhere it was reported that a foreigner had bought many antiques from Tibetans, but due to the influence of a spiritual person who remained anonymous, he had left them in the hands of an unknown beneficiary or arranged to have them returned to the authorities.

Did Gem know about this foreigner? customers at the hotel asked.

"I never deal with foreigners. Besides, they come and stay at big hotels that have their own guides," Gem replied.

If there was a mischievous glint in his eyes when he said that, it was just the customers' imagination. Gem always squinted in the sun, and the sun was always shining in his eyes.

This Time Goat;
Next Time Man

The Nanjangud narrow gauge train left for Arsikere in
the early hours of the morning with its annual burden
of pilgrims to the Tirumalai hills packed into its
matchbox cabins. It took all day to travel the hundred-
odd miles, sometimes with delays between stations
where villagers with no means to carry their harvest of
vegetables would block the tracks with their bamboo
baskets. Many of them had become expert train-top
riders, contentedly perching on top of the cars along
with their tomatoes, cabbages, eggplants, mint leaves,
and even chickens. After all, the Nanjangud narrow
gauge's top speed—which it never reached—was only
thirty miles per hour.

At Arsikere things changed. Medium and broad
gauge tracks commanded the main platform, which
was reached by overpass from the small stationmaster's hut where the Nanjangud train came to a dead

end. It was sad to see the narrow gauge train standing all alone after the passengers had deserted it, its steam trailing into the air thinner than the smoke of a cigarette. It would wait there until the next morning, when it would return to the small town of Nanjangud.

Pandu, the train singer, usually slept until he reached Arsikere. His singing worked best on broad gauge trains, where the cars were spacious and the pace of motion was swift. The pilgrims became impassive, and the singer's tunes, almost in harmony with the swaying of the train, relaxed them. Pandu studied his customers carefully. If the men were reading newspapers and their womenfolk were sitting on the wooden berths with their legs pulled up, it was a car for devotionals. If the men wore pants and the women wore nylon saris and carried stainless steel thermoses, he sang film songs. An artist creates his tunes to suit the stage, he would say. Besides, if one wasn't prepared with a versatile repertoire, how could one survive? When Pandu found one of his songs getting stale, he would write new lyrics, change the melody, and try it out on some unsuspecting passenger. But on the broad gauge train to the Tirumalai hills, he knew it had to be mostly devotional lyrics and bhajans of saints if he were to come out with a profit.

Mathew, the engine driver to the hills, waited in Anwar's refreshment stall until the train was full. He had parked his engine—the famous Pilgrimage Carrier No. 904—at a distance from the cars, until ten minutes before departure. He had polished 904's face until the brass numbers shone and the red painted disc on the front looked freshly painted. Now he sipped his tea at the broken glass window of the stall in his polka-dot shirt and green scarf. Mathew was the Clark Gable of Arsikere and the only engineer to drive No. 904. When pilgrims landed in Arsikere, they would ask the station staff which engine was going to pull them to the hills. If the answer was No. 904, they had another reason (in addition to their holy mission) to rejoice, for No. 904 never went without Mathew and Mathew never failed to deliver his cargo safely to its destination. And Mathew drove the pilgrimage train at fifty miles per hour, come curve, tunnel, or bridge. No one even thought of asking No. 904 to stop anywhere except where Mathew did, at the destined stations.

When Mathew stepped out of the biryani stall, Pandu busied himself behind a magazine. But having heard the way Mathew cleared his throat while passing behind him, Pandu knew he had been seen, which meant that at Bangarpet, when the train stopped for lunch, he would have to sing Pat Boone or Ricky Nelson to Mathew in the engineer's car. Pandu didn't know the songs well and Mathew had the irksome habit of correcting his accent, to the amusement of the signal guard, the stationmaster, and the Anglo-Indian lady who brought Mathew plum cakes on blue plates covered with white handmade brocade. Pandu was a born singer, but when it came to English songs, Mathew with his rum-tempered voice could put Pandu's seventeen years of singing to shame. Mathew enjoyed this confrontation, especially when Susy, his porcelain plate lady, was around.

"I can sing better than you any day!" Mathew would say while Susy fondled his ear and he nibbled on her pink fingernails as if crumbs from the plum cake still lingered there.

Pandu knew that Mathew meant well. He didn't have to buy a ticket if 904 was the engine on any route. In fact, when Pandu sang some of the Hindi film tunes that Mathew liked, he could see a soft glow on the engine driver's face. At times Mathew would lament, "If I had been born in England or in America, I'd have been a singer and an actor instead of being cursed to this fate of engine driving."

"But look what would have happened to engine 904 if you weren't here to drive it! You're a hero in the eyes of millions of passengers. When they see you in your red engine, they cheer and wave. You're almost a saint to them," Pandu would say to cheer him up.

"Fancy that," Mathew would chuckle. "An Anglo-Indian playing saint to all these Hindoos on their way to a stone god up on top of a junglee hill!"

On this day, Pandu launched himself onto the side of a second-class compartment as the train slowly pulled out of the station. He kept a wary eye on the ticket collector, who sometimes hung on to the other side of the train to surprise free riders. As the train gathered speed, Pandu let himself in and quickly surveyed the occupants. An elderly man in a closed-collar shirt sat sipping coffee from a stainless steel tumbler. A lawyer, perhaps. Next to him sat a pretty lady in her early twenties with a stack of magazines. Across from them was an elderly woman busily unwrapping her bags. On the other side of the passageway, a newly married couple sat stiffly separate from each other. They must have been disappointed that the second-class compartment was not empty.

Pandu started to sing. He began with a romantic popular song with some reference to destiny having the upper hand in matters of the heart. The elderly man gave him a quick look. The pretty lady, who was definitely his daughter, smiled and in a half-innocent manner tapped her foot. The newly marrieds turned red in the face. At least a few rupees were in the bag. But the elderly lady, who had already shown her disapproval by craning her neck out the window for signs of the ticket collector, was the one he had to soften up. Pandu quickly ended the first song and switched to an old devotional. He sang it with fervor, holding his hands in supplication to the roof of the compartment, as though God sat on top of it, listening. The elderly lady was in ecstasy. Tears welled up in her eyes as she nodded her head to each and every word of the dialogue between a dying saint and his God. Pandu finished the bhajan and asked if there were any requests. The elderly lady asked him to sing another old bhajan, one even illiterate beggars knew. Pandu began while the lady browsed in her bag, which was thick with rupees. The newly marrieds were already holding rupees in their hands for him. Mathew blew the whistle three times to indicate they were approaching Bangarpet. The day looked promising.

Before the train could come to a halt, Pandu jumped out from the back of the compartment with his loot. There had been no need to be so cautious, however. The ticket collector was not a new man, as he had feared, but an old fan of his.

"Hey Pandu, you were singing pretty good from what I could hear," he yelled from the window as Pandu walked toward the engine.

Mathew emerged from No. 904 with a box in his hand.

"You don't have to bore me today with your accent," he said with a wink. "This is Susy's birthday, so I'm going over to her place."

Partly relieved that he didn't have to sing English songs for Mathew and partly annoyed because he had practiced a Dean Martin song all night to surprise him, Pandu entered the Bangarpet platform.

He couldn't believe what he saw. The facade of the ticket office was freshly painted, and garlands of flowers hung in the arches. The staff all wore freshly ironed uniforms, and the sweeper had cleaned and sprinkled the walkways with fresh sand. The national flag was fluttering on its mast, and in the waiting room next to the canteen sat a handsome young man dressed in khaki, his thick black crop of hair neatly combed to the side. On the table next to him was a tray of tea and cigarettes. He was whispering something in the ear of the superintendent of police, who had waxed his belt and holster to shine like glass. His khaki uniform was starched to glow in its stiffness as he stood beside the town's elders, lawyer Lingappa, Municipality President Pandit, and the town doctor, Murthy.

"In America, you wouldn't believe how clean they keep their railway and bus stations. Not a scrap of rubbish anywhere. We must improve our hygiene and our outlook. Our public places should shine like our bodies. Public impressions are so important. It's our foreign-exchange earner!" said the handsome young man.

Everyone nodded and a few even applauded. Pandu wasn't certain how public impressions earned foreign exchange. Across from the waiting room, Betta's she-goat was pissing loudly on the new sand that the sweeper had sprinkled. Catching sight of Pandu, Doctor Murthy averted the embarrassment.

"Pandu! Come in! Let me introduce you to Dr. Siddhu, our party's choice in the coming elections, not to mention our new chief minister!" he said, and turning to Dr. Siddhu, he explained, "Pandu is our train singer, one of the best. He sings both Indian and English songs."

Dr. Siddhu looked amused. He placed his cup and saucer on the table and lit a cigarette.

"With an accent, of course!" he muttered.

The entourage laughed. It was a hot afternoon and Pandu was hungry.

"I haven't eaten all day," he said.

"Neither have I," replied Dr. Siddhu. "Besides, it's best to sing on a hungry stomach. Once you load yourself up, you'll croak!" His gold fillings sparkled when he laughed.

"I don't sing on Fridays," Pandu said.

"Why not? What's the occasion?" Dr. Siddhu no longer looked amused.

"The occasion is one of my own. Once a week I do not sing, to keep my voice clean and without rubbish!"

Dr. Siddhu caught the message.

"You're an insolent young man. It's not becoming in a person who makes his living singing on trains."

He drew the police superintendent's attention and whispered something to him. Betta's she-goat had now joined the crowd on the platform and, seeing one of the posters featuring Dr. Siddhu's picture peeling from the wall, began to nibble it.

Pandu, feeling that the matter of his confrontation with the party's choice was over, went to the biryani stall. Before he had a chance to swallow a mouthful of rice, the superintendent materialized with two constables.

"I'm taking you into custody," he said.

"On what offense?" Pandu asked.

"Traveling without a ticket," the Superintendent said, and motioned to the constables to shackle his hands. Pandu was led to the police jeep waiting outside the station. As he rode, Pandu noticed that the politician's face was all over town on big banners and posters. All the rich and influential town elders were supporting him against the local candidate, a high school teacher who had been branded by the wealthy as a no-good socialist. The assistant superintendent received him at the station and led him to his cell. "You should have behaved yourself," he said.

The police station was a very small building with two rooms—one used as the main office and the other partitioned by iron bars into two cells for offenders.

Pandu's cell directly faced the desk where the superintendent sat. The assistant superintendent didn't even have his own desk, but sat opposite the superintendent in a chair. It was like one big family. Pandu could also see through the front entrance to the empty main street. The assistant superintendent's bicycle leaned against the station's brick compound. One of the constables who had arrested him sat on a small stool at the gate, dozing. A few passersby who could see inside by standing at the gate were pointing at him and talking.

It had been two hours since his arrest, and Pandu fell into an exhausted, hungry nap. He dreamed he was back on the train in the same compartment. The elderly lady had laid a feast in front of him and joined in singing while they all ate. The daughter, playfully hiding behind a magazine, was winking at him. The father, a lawyer, was taking his family on a pilgrimage to the hills. He thought Pandu would make a fine bridegroom for his daughter and was proposing a marriage, when Pandu was rudely awakened by shouting between the superintendent and the assistant.

"That Anglo, Mathew, is a son-of-a bitch. Wait till I get my hands on him," swore the superintendent.

"I told you a long time ago I needed a motorbike, not a bicycle. When you are away with the jeep, I've no way of getting anywhere fast enough in an emergency!" the assistant complained.

Pandu looked out. More than a few curious onlookers had gathered around and their group was growing larger as the supporters of the high school teacher joined in to canvas votes for their candidate. Naturally, they showed sympathy for Pandu's situation. Two young men, obviously students of the teacher, began to shout, "Release Pandu, Go Home, Siddhu."

"It's all your fault!" said the superintendent, suddenly turning to glare at Pandu.

The constable who had been dozing in the front hours before came hurrying back. He must have pedaled the assistant's bicycle at breakneck speed: sweat trickled from his forehead, and when he took his turban off, sweat poured from all sides of his face.

"Did you find him?"

"No, sir. It seems he's away in Bangalore on family business," replied the constable, collapsing on the floor.

"If I were not a reasonable man, I'd teach you a lesson to remember," the assistant yelled at Pandu.

It was a nightmare. Pandu could hardly follow what was happening. After the constable sufficiently recovered from his exhaustion, both the superintendent and the assistant left in a huff. The constable filled Pandu in on the events. When Mathew heard what had happened to Pandu, he had approached Dr. Siddhu and the police on Pandu's behalf, but they had refused to accept his explanation. Mathew had then driven the train with the politician in it out of Bangarpet. Then, a few miles out of town, he had brought the train to a sudden stop on the perilous bridge over the Janaki River. Half the train was past the wooden bridge, which was too narrow for passengers to walk on when the train occupied it. The only way for the passengers in front to get back to Bangarpet would be to climb down the steep canyon and swim. Dr. Siddhu, it turned out, could not swim. He was also afraid of heights and refused to leave his first-class cabin. The Janaki River bridge was a hot political issue each year around election time, though after the elections no one seemed to care about repairing it. Built in the era of British rule, it had deteriorated to such a degree that crossing it had become an adventure. Mathew had said that one of the pistons on the big wheel was malfunctioning. He needed time to fix it. The only other man who knew anything about fixing train wheels, a relative of Mathew, was out of town.

"Conveniently, you might say," thought the constable. "I knocked on his door and his wife said he was away in Bangalore. Maybe he was inside hiding!"

Pandu heard Doctor Murthy's Morris pull up in front of the station. The car was full of the town's dignitaries. It was amazing that so many could fit in such a small car.

The doctor approached Pandu. "Pandu, I have known you for so many years. How many times have I helped you! How many times have I mentioned your name to passing movie producers! You must help us now."

"What is it you want me to do? I've been arrested and held in jail. I know how to sing on trains, not how to fix broken engines," Pandu said with open sarcasm.

Doctor Murthy ignored it. "If you'll prevail over your friend Mathew to somehow give up this bluff and drive the train to the hills, we'll see that you're released," he said. The others nodded their heads reassuringly.

Outside the police station, someone shouted that it was unfair to treat a poor train singer this way. Another held up a sign that read, "Down with the Congress party!"

"I want an apology from your politician, Dr. Siddhu," Pandu replied. "I want him to say that he was sorry to have insulted me at the station."

"What nonsense! You were arrested for traveling without a ticket. Dr. Siddhu had nothing to do with it. You think a foreign-returned dignitary who might well become our chief minister would write an apology to a train singer? You're out of your mind."

The crowd outside had increased. The pilgrims who were on the safe side of the bridge had walked into town and joined the agitation. Many were women and children. The superintendent, who had now returned, posted the constables and the assistant outside to calm them.

"You'll have your pilgrimage. Please go back to the station" was the plea. By sunset, the crowd had not dispersed. The high school teacher had arrived with a new batch of students. He wanted to speak to Pandu.

"You're a brave man. You have shown the Congress party it cannot simply have its way just because all the wealthy and influential are on its side. Please join our opposition," he pleaded.

The lawyer to whose family Pandu had sung now appeared inside the station. He was quite annoyed with the whole situation. "We are on a pilgrimage, not on a local sight-seeing tour," he said to the superintendent. "I've heard the young man sing. He's a god-fearing man. So what if he was traveling without a ticket? We will pay his fine. You must release him and let us proceed with our pilgrimage instead of using this situation to harass us."

The crowd, which had moved inside the gate despite the request of the constables, cheered the lawyer. Some waved at Pandu. Since nightfall, the pilgrims had camped in front of the station. Banners appeared from nowhere with slogans like LET THE TRAIN SINGER FREE! and DOWN WITH DICTATORS! Some even shouted that they'd attack the station if Pandu were not released by midnight.

Doctor Murthy and the superintendent kept shunting between the stranded train and the police station in the Morris. News came that the train guard, who had been assigned to carry food across the bridge because of his ability to hang onto the train railings, had slipped into the river with the food. Luckily, he was a good swimmer and had managed to get back to the station. He now refused to do any more balancing on the bridge. Dr. Siddhu was left without anything to eat. Doctor Murthy had swum across to the politician with Pandu's demands but the politician had refused to apologize. By nine in the evening, an automobile belonging to the politician's party had arrived with men who looked like wrestlers. The stalemate was on.

It was around four in the morning when someone woke the constable and said he wished to speak with

Pandu. It was Mathew. His eyes were bloodshot. Pandu could smell rum. He was relieved to see that his friend was all right.

"What's the matter with the pistons on No. 904?" he asked.

"The same thing that's the matter with pride," replied Mathew, and winked.

They sat together, each reminiscing about his life. Finally, Mathew broached the subject of the day's events.

"You know, you have won a victory over this Siddhu and his powerful party. The high school teacher thinks that he can win the election with your help. But I tell you, the politician is not going to apologize. I don't want to sit here and cause more trouble to my passengers or to the train schedules. Why don't you tell them that you'll let bygones be bygones, and I'll agree to fix the engine?"

Pandu was tired. There was no sense in insisting on something that was not going to happen, no matter how much it was justified. Maybe this was the time he was destined to pay for all the free rides, though he had never dreamed it would be with imprisonment.

The superintendent arrived within minutes when Pandu sent word. Doctor Murthy hopped into his Morris and went to the bridge with the good news. The pilgrims were relieved.

"Anytime you need anything, you just come to me," said the lawyer, who was now their spokesman.

The town elders stood in line with the police as Pandu was released. They looked tired and old without their leader. The jeep took Mathew and Pandu to the bank of the Janaki River. Mathew stopped on the way to gather assorted wrenches and two young boys to assist him in repairing the pistons. If everyone knew that Mathew was bluffing, no one dared to say so. The three swam easily to the other side of the river while pilgrims on both sides cheered them. The first-class compartment where Dr. Siddhu waited showed no signs of life. Once they reached the engine, Mathew dismissed his young assistants, who left laughing. He fooled around with the pistons, making a lot of racket and banging his hammer loud enough to send echoes across the canyon. After an hour of such fooling around, Mathew turned to Pandu.

"I think it's best you stay in Bangarpet. You're a hero now, and something will come of it. Maybe this is your chance to take advantage of the situation and make something out of your life."

"What about you?" asked Pandu. He was thinking of what Dr. Siddhu in his wrath might do to harm Mathew when he returned from the pilgrimage.

"I'm a survivor," Mathew replied. "I know how to keep one step ahead of these egotists. Besides, India is full of trains!"

Mathew gave Pandu a warm hug, then quickly climbed into his seat. He gave the whistle a long, victorious tug. The engine slowly began to move. Pandu could hear passengers clapping, some chanting slogans that the train singer was the hero of the incident. The first-class compartment passed by, but the politician had pulled down the shades. Perhaps he was busy rehearsing his version of the incident in Bangarpet for the newspapers.

Pandu was sad that he was not back on the train singing for the passengers, making the day mean nothing beyond the simple, fulfilling pleasure of being alive. In a matter of one day, things had changed so drastically that he couldn't even recall why his sincere answer to the politician had ended in a confrontation affecting so many lives. He remembered one of his favorite bhajans, that said man does not make destiny; destiny chooses man to fulfill itself. Strange words, but in the context of what had happened to him, he could feel there was something to those words after all. As he walked back to Bangarpet, Pandu tried to examine all the songs he knew to see if there were any others that explained the mysteries of life even better. By the time he reached the outer limits of the town, a small crowd had gathered around the Three Lights Circle, so called because it was at the junction of three roads, one leading to Bangalore, the capital of the state, another to the local burial grounds, and the third, winding through small villages and miles and miles of wilderness, to Nanjangud, his home town.

He recognized Betta immediately. Betta made way for him to enter the circling crowd.

"Look, Pandu. Look what the big people have done to my mother goat," he said, as tears rolled down his wrinkled, old cheeks.

In the center, with her forelegs on the small cement platform that supported the Three Lights, as if trying to find cover in its sanctuary, the she-goat lay. Her hind legs were broken. Blood ran out of her partly open mouth, over her limp tongue, onto the cement. The body was still warm.

"She breathed her last just a few minutes ago," said Betta. "She was still alive until I came here. She knew it was me when I touched her. She bleated her last in my hands."

Pandu could see tire marks over her back.

"It was the politician's automobile that came into town with those goondas when you were in the lock-up," said a bystander. "I recognized it. It was speeding to the capital with the congress flag on its hood."

They gently carried the she-goat to the burial ground. Word was sent for the local priest to come and perform the ceremonies. As they waited, the local citizens gathered one by one in the burial ground. There were many who knew the goat, who had drunk her milk and nursed their children on it. Pandu remembered how she used to come to him when the train stopped and wait gently until he had eaten his lunch. Then she would nibble the banana leaf from his hands and lick his palm, as if to thank him. After the burial, a group of elders surrounded him. The school teacher was among them.

"We have come to the decision that you, instead of our school teacher, should stand in opposition to Dr. Siddhu," they said.

Pandu was dumbfounded. He had no experience in politics.

"There is no need to feel unworthy. What matters is what you stand for. We know what you stood for when you confronted Dr. Siddhu. We know how much you loved the goat. We want someone who stands for our pride and our dignity."

On the day he was to speak to the people of Bangarpet, the road to the Three Lights Circle was festooned as if for the arrival of an important potentate. Posters carrying his picture hung in front of shops and on the bare walls of buildings and cinema halls. At the circle, a small platform had been built and a life-sized papier-mâché figure of Betta's goat was installed. Pandu was amazed at the crowd that had gathered. Even the townsmen who supported Dr. Siddhu were there, if not to support Pandu, then at least to listen to what he might say. The two constables who had shackled Pandu now stood guarding the platform. Though he could not see the superintendent, he saw the assistant standing in front of the jeep. As soon as Pandu approached the platform with his benefactors and with those who had taken up the task of apprising him on matters with which he was not familiar, a group of students encircled him and hoisted him over their shoulders. There was thunderous applause.

Pandu felt a sudden exultation. Words that had previously seemed inaccessible and alien now formed in his mind. He felt a strange, giddy sense of power. He could barely hear the school teacher make his introductory speech. People he had never known came in droves to garland him or touch him, as if he were a holy man. Then it was time for him to take the microphone. He paused for the cheers and applause to die down, then, holding the microphone close to his mouth, he began.

Moneylenders

Seth Tej was rich, but the dilapidated tenement in which he lived did not show it. He owned the building. In fact, he owned all the dilapidated buildings on the lane. It was named after him by word of mouth, though it possessed another older name, according to the stone inscription embedded into the wall. Even the mailman delivered mail addressed to Seth Tej Lane. Seth Tej lived on the upper story of this three-storied building. He rented the other two to families who belonged to his own caste. Seth Tej was a moneylender, and when I went to him with my complaint about the condition of the overground drainage in front of his house, he was receiving gifts and congratulations from his tenants on his coming marriage. He was in his late thirties, bald and obese. As my supervisor had said, I found him willing to listen to what I had to say.

I'm a clerk at the municipality. I'd been recently posted to supervise sanitary conditions in Seth Tej Lane. The drainage gutter was full of trash. Amid the accumulated garbage that sat in the gutter, growing higher, there were stagnant pools of foul-smelling water. Rats freely moved from one stinking heap to the next like otters.

"I shall take care of this," said Seth Tej, after asking me who I worked for and how much I earned. Seth Tej sat on the front porch of his house on a soft, soiled cushion with a swatter in hand. He offered me the sweets on a plate from which he was eating. Around the plate lay a few dead flies.

"You come tomorrow, you'll see the gutter clean," he said, while focusing his eyes on my wristwatch.

"Best to leave things as they are," said my supervisor when I reported to him the next day that all Seth Tej had done was to throw buckets of water over the garbage, thus moving the heaps a little farther away from his house toward the next tenement. My supervisor lived on Seth Tej Lane. I paid the street scavenger extra to clear the heaps.

On the next month's inspection rounds, Seth Tej was sitting in front of his house with a very young, pretty woman. As soon as he saw me, he asked her to pull her sari over her head. I later heard that Seth Tej had stopped his wife from strolling down his street without a hooded sari. A maid now accompanied her. The drainage gutter was clogged as before.

"You're wasting your time on this," said Tej. "This garbage is not unsanitary. Besides, there's no other place for my tenants to throw stuff. Come monsoon, everything will be washed out to the river."

I'm a grown man. I've been recently promoted. I understand and bow to the higher order of bureaucracy.

When I was a student, I was a freedom fighter. My
teachers thought I'd some day turn communist. At
some point as I grew up, I realized that the world was
very large. Unknown powers shaped man's destiny, but
the rich and the influential controlled mine. I prepared
my report: "Inspected Seth Tej Lane. Matter of garbage in drainage dealt with by landlord. Problem
caused more by nature than by neglect. Sanitation sat-
isfactory." Unfair?

My supervisor nodded his head with approval. "It's
just a minor matter. When you need money, go to
Seth Tej. He'll remember!"

Next month, my father died. Since he didn't have any
life insurance, his burial expenses drained me of my
savings. On top of this, my wife fell ill and had to be
admitted to a nursing clinic. I was suddenly flat broke.

My supervisor introduced me to a new man who had
arrived in town. His name was Seth Romi. He had just
joined the club I frequented. Seth Romi was in his
mid-twenties. He was well built and handsome. He
was opening his own moneylending business.

"I heard that you've some money problems. Come to
my shop and I'll loan you twice as much as anybody
else on your articles," he said. I don't know if he had
heard of Tej, who had been the only moneylender until
Romi arrived. I cheered up, thinking that at last there
was somebody who would give Seth Tej some competition. But would one Seth cross the other?

Later, when we broke up the party, Seth Romi drew
me aside. "Tell me, what do you think of Seth Tej's
wife?"

"She's very beautiful, but no one sees her anymore!"

"She's more than beautiful! She's a goddess, a goddess, I tell you," Romi chanted somewhat in stupor. He pleaded with me to stay a little longer.

"He stole her from me with his bags of money. We were in love, roaming in the parks hand in hand. It's so unfair, unfair!" Romi lamented over the beer.

"All's fair in love and war," I said.

"Never, never!" declared Romi.

When I took the family gold to Seth Romi, he was a changed man.

"I'm sorry. You must go to Seth Tej. I'm a newcomer here and he has the first option," said Seth Romi, averting his eyes from my bewildered stare.

"But the other day . . ." I began.

"A mistake," he concluded. "We are in this business as brothers. Brothers in caste, brothers in tradition. He'll be quite fair," Romi said with ease. His eyes were all business.

"So you went to my competitor, I hear! So you thought you could get a better loan!" Seth Tej exclaimed, as he weighed the gold in his tiny scales. The clerk made notes in his ledger and drew up a loan paper with interest rates and deductions already made from the loan for the first month's interest. The money Tej offered was ridiculous. I refused to pawn my gold.

"Where else can you take it?" Seth Tej asked, laughing. As I left, I saw him reach for the telephone.

When I arrived at Seth Romi's shop, he made me wait until all the others had left. Then he went through my gold with the usual appraisal.

"I'm sorry, I cannot accept this," he said, as if I were a stranger.

"Why?" I asked, growing angrier by the minute. "Did Seth Tej call you? Are you afraid of the man who stole your sweetheart?"

"Please, not so loud," urged Seth Romi, looking quickly at the street. "This is business. Now that Seth Tej has told you what it's worth, all I can do is to offer you less. Everything else is irrelevant!"

"In that case, I'll take it back to Seth Tej!"

"That'll do you no good. He'll refuse to give you anything. When that happens and you come back to me, I'll have to do the same!" Romi said, and smiled with wisdom. I wanted to hit him. Seeing my intentions clearly on my face, he changed his expression.

"All isn't fair in love or war, eh?" I said when I completed the transaction.

"You've got it!" Romi smiled triumphantly. "It's only fair in literature. Life is business, not literature!" he said.

I went to the club that night. Seth Tej was there with my supervisor and a couple of others. I bought them all a second round of drinks, and when the waiter came with the bill, I unrolled my wad of notes to pay him. I ordered the best whiskey and cigarettes for myself. Seth Tej squirmed in his seat and kept looking at my shirt pocket, where I kept my folded bills. His eyes were trying to count them! I lit a cigarette and blew the smoke into his face. Seth Tej batted the smoke from his face and laughed congenially at my antic.

"Did my competition pay you more?" he asked.

I kept smoking my cigarette and blowing rings over his head. Seth Tej tried his best to keep his face free of agitation, but it was showing. He finished his drink.

"The next round is yours!" I said, and looked at the others, who nodded.

Tej wiped his face with his kerchief.

"I'll go in and order the drinks," he said trying to get up.

"No, no, don't trouble yourself," I replied, and pulled him down as I beckoned for the waiter.

"Another round here, on Seth Tej this time. Make mine the same as before," I said to the waiter, pointing to my whiskey. Tej let out a deep sigh and searched for his wallet.

"Is Romi coming here tonight?" he asked at last.

"I thought both of you would be here together!" I replied.

"Why?"

"Well, I saw Romi walking toward your house almost an hour ago. The way he was dressed, I thought there was some celebration at your place!" I bluffed as casually as I could.

Seth Tej moved closer and gripped my arm.

"Did you say you saw him going to my house an hour ago?"

"Yes. Maybe it was an hour and a half ago! He told me he knew your wife's family. After all, he's from her hometown!"

Seth Tej wasn't listening to my words. He kept looking at his diamond-studded watch and saying to

himself, "It's now two hours!" Once or twice he made
an attempt to get up from the chair, but the whiskey
had taken its possessive grip of his head after saturat-
ing the fat in his body. He slumped back, glad of the
dark in the veranda where we sat. I could only imagine the lizard-like twitches that shot through his face.
The club stereo played popular movie songs about
unrequited love or passion. In between the songs,
Seth Tej would exclaim, "Unfair, so unfair," and everyone sitting at the table nodded their heads in approval
of Seth Tej's sentiment.

Maya

Maya in its diverse forms tempts the human eye to different conclusions, but sculptors know that it is by prevailing over the confusion it creates in the mind that one overcomes its spell. Duality has been a key to the achievement of a purer vision.

In the ancient temple of Nanjangud, the old masters had carved many interpretations of Maya. The hundreds of deities that surrounded the inner sanctuary of Shiva in seeming chaos were only meant to cleanse the mind in preparation for the purer vision inside of the formless black stone of godhood. But in the courtyard of the temple, the old masters had gone ecstatic. On the black marble pillar that stood in the middle of the quadrangle, nymphs and demons, at once hideous and graceful, danced round and round in an ascending spiral until their limbs, their faces, their gestures, all blended in on themselves. A dark softness, deeper than the marble itself, absorbed their dualities, silence prevailed over illusion, over life's unforgiving deceptions, leaving a calm, eternal oneness.

It was payday. Sheshadri, on his way back home, stopped at the temple. He loved to gaze for hours at the pillar. Although he desperately wished he understood what the old masters had been trying to say, the concept of duality was something he still wrestled with. He had derived much inspiration for the carvings he was commissioned to do on the new town hall from the pillar, but the town patriarchs had insisted that the nymphs and demons he carved present a clear interpretation of good and evil. They wanted the nymphs to have the faces of movie stars and the demons to be as ugly and inhuman as possible. They wanted no hint or suggestion of one being part of the other.

Sheshadri paused at the parrot astrologer under the banyan tree and for a rupee had the parrot pull out a card of fate. The parrot, half starved, feigned to scan all the soiled cards, then held one out in its beak. The astrologer read it. Extraordinary turn of events, prosperity, long life. There was no mention of happiness.

The nymph he would carve would be unlike the ones the masters had carved. She'd be slender in her breasts and ankle, light-limbed, quick in her gesturing eye. As he walked home, he passed by a huge brick wall whose plaster had developed many cracks. A crow sat next to one rain-sodden crack. Suddenly an insect emerged. The crow caught it. The insect wriggled its legs all over the crow's beak as it was being methodically swallowed. Sheshadri remembered a fable his grandmother used to tell. By the curse of an enraged rishi, a nymph was once turned into a crow. Eventually, when the spell was lifted, the nymph had emerged with two heads, one of her former self, the other of a fierce brooding sister. He had forgotten the rest of the story. He crossed the street near the busy intersection of his neighborhood. A city bus honked furiously at his transgression.

His father met him at the door. There were visitors. Fruits and a silver platter full of sweets sat on the table. A man as old as his father rose from the chair.

"This is Lakpathy from Gubbi," his father introduced the old man who wore many rings on his hands. His mouth was almost devoid of teeth; the few that remained glittered with their fillings of gold.

"Mr. Lakpathy is the zamindar of Gubbi. He has come to see your sister! It's only God's grace that such a fortune has befallen us."

Behind the kitchen door, Sheshadri could sense some strange women. They withdrew farther into the kitchen before he could see any of their faces.

"Mr. Lakpathy has brought us many gifts," added his father, trying to gain his attention. Sheshadri saw the large bamboo basket that sat in a corner. There were several silk saris, boxes of velvet, and a valise that was bulging obviously with money.

"Your sister has already given her consent!" said Mr. Lakpathy, as if he sensed what was going on in Sheshadri's mind, and nervously cracked his knuckles. They sounded like brittle twigs on fire.

"Then what are you waiting for me to say?" quipped Sheshadri, confused and angry.

"You had better go inside, my son. Your mother would like to have a word with you," hastened his

father, trying to cover his embarrassment with a
smile.

Sheshadri's mother was waiting in the backyard.
His sister, face bent, sat under the champak tree. It
was old now and barely produced a blossom or two in
its season. Sheshadri remembered how, when he was
a boy, he used to climb up the tree and shake the fragrant white flowers over his sister's head.

"Son, this is our only chance. As you know, no one
has come to ask for your sister—we are neither rich
nor is she blessed with a light complexion. Time is
slipping by. This man, maybe he's old and has been
married before, but he's willing to marry her. He's rich
and will take care of her. Besides, he says he'll give
you whatever you wish if you'll marry his daughter!"
His mother pointed toward the window in the
kitchen. Sheshadri caught a glimpse of the old man's
daughter before she withdrew quickly.

Suddenly, all his anger at the old man's audacity
melted. She was enchanting! The face he glimpsed
was the one he had been dreaming about for his
nymph. He could not believe this strange happening.
Why were all these arrangements being made behind
his back? Was the old man using his daughter as a
pawn for his own gain?

"The old man believes in astrology. He said that the
reason why his previous wife died from a mysterious
sickness was because she had not followed religious
advice. He says that his astrologer wants it to be a
double marriage, and the bridegroom for his daughter
must come from the house of the one he chooses to

be his bride, and the marriages, to be holy and long-lasting, have to take place at exactly the same place and time," explained his mother.

A double marriage! Odd these days, but Sheshadri respected astral beliefs. How else could it be that he was gaining such a goddess? But he wondered about his sister. Would she be happy married to such an old goat? He looked at her but did not have the courage to ask. Clear stars shone above. A lizard twitched its tail over the doorsill. Taking his silence as his consent, his mother and sister had already disappeared into the kitchen. He could hear them animatedly talking with the rest. There was much laughter and rejoicing. As he re-entered the house, he caught sight of a dark woman, heavy and slow in her motions, move away from his sight. She must have been watching him. Perhaps a servant girl of the guests.

The guests left before sunrise. Now the basket of gifts was theirs. His father happily sat on the chair counting the money. His mother was praising the quality and richness of the saris. His sister was trying them on.

"A double marriage! A thing of the past these days. But I hope you'll soon be back to finish the double sculptures!" joked the temple trustee when he heard the news.

The old man of Gubbi was indeed the wealthiest in town. The town was decorated as if it was getting ready to receive the prime minister. Lakpathy's two-storied gabled house was decorated with the traditional mango and banana leaves. Marigolds and garlands of chrysanthemum hung everywhere. In the hall, the

ritual homa before which he and Lakpathy would tie
the thali were built opposite to each other. Everything
had been duplicated exactly.

The wedding ceremonies began late in the afternoon. The bridegrooms, seated opposite, went
through many required rituals of purification before
the brides were escorted to join them. It was almost
dusk before the priests completed the preliminaries
and sent word for the brides. Lakpathy had many
brass lamps lit for the occasion, though the house had
electricity. The lamps cast a romantic haze, and in
their glow, the priests looked holier than usual. As the
brides, bedecked in silk and jewelry, their saris
hooded over their faces, were escorted to the wooden
seats in front of Sheshadri and Lakpathy, the priests
held the ritual curtain in front of the bridegrooms. It
was at the moment of tying the thali when the sacred
curtain was lowered and the brides and the grooms
saw each other as man and wife forever. Sheshadri
cast a shy look at Lakpathy, whose sacred curtain was
white and quite transparent. He wondered why his
was black and opaque, though it was more elaborately
embroidered. The brides arrived to the sound of
drums and were seated on the other side of the curtains. The priests began chanting the last mantra that
would solemnize the wedlock, and then to the height-
ened accompaniment of instruments, they slowly
lowered the curtains while nodding at the bridegrooms who stood with the sacred thali in their
hands, ready to tie them around the neck of their
brides. Sheshadri could hear his heart pounding. A

goddess sat there inches away from his hand and in a moment or so, she would be his forever! Hers would be the face that would embellish the town hall, hers would be the grace, the smile. Sheshadri felt the priest nudging him. The curtains were down and the drums were beating in a wild climax for the tying of the thali. Sheshadri carefully leaned over and his bride lifted her head to receive the thali. And Sheshadri suddenly froze! He could not believe what he saw. She was not the one he had seen in the kitchen window! She was the servant girl!

"You're a man, Sheshu," pleaded his father, who had suddenly appeared beside him. "Dakshi here is the sister of Neema who you saw in our house. Though they were born to separate mothers, they're both Lakpathy's daughters and inherit his wealth equally. What if she's not pretty? She's an excellent cook, seamstress, and housekeeper!"

"No!" screamed Sheshadri. His hand shook uncontrollably. Dakshi sat under his quivering hand like a buffalo ready for the sacrifice.

"My son," whispered his mother, who had joined to plead with his father. "Mr. Lakpathy will not marry your sister unless you tie the thali. Your sister will kill herself in shame. Do you think I'd live with such a disgrace over my head? Do you wish to destroy all of us?"

"Think, my son," rejoined his father, wiping his forehead with a towel, growing paler each second. "It was Neema's idea that it should be this way. She will not marry anyone until her sister is married. They're like twins, bone and marrow. You're not losing anything.

Neema will come to see her sister, and she'll be in your debt forever. You'll have enough wealth to do anything you want. You're a man!"

Sheshadri looked at Lakpathy, who held his thali over his sister's head while she wept. He looked victorious, a corrupt smile slowly spreading over his face. Those gathered in the hall had their eyes transfixed on Sheshadri. No one moved. Sheshadri felt a shiver run down his spine. He knew he held in his hand, for that single moment, the gesture that would carve their destinies.

As Sheshadri tied the thali, the guests heaved a sigh of relief. Some even applauded. A tear fell softly on his arm.

"God does things in his own way, though he lets us think we are our own masters. My prophecy was accurate," said the parrot astrologer.

Sheshadri resigned himself to his fate. He left the house earlier than usual and stayed out late. Dakshi quietly waited for him with the food and would not eat until he had. She slept on a coir mat away from their nuptial bed. Except for one or two drunken nights, Sheshadri did not speak to her, yet she knew what pleased him most. There was a fresh towel by his bedside when he woke and a cup of coffee waiting when he finished his bath. One holiday he heard Dakshi singing in the backyard with a haunting, beautiful voice. But the face that had dazzled him from the kitchen window always returned to disturb his thoughts.

When he heard that Neema's father Lakpathy was proposing her marriage to Babu, the town temple trustee's son, he was inflamed. Babu was a playboy, a debaucher and gambler. He asked Dakshi to inform her sister. When he heard that Neema had gladly given her consent to the marriage, he felt betrayed. He refused to participate in their wedding.

After the wedding in Gubbi, Babu threw a lavish reception at Nanjangud.

"My father has told me that you're looking for a face for the temple carvings. You should see my wife. She'll put any goddess to shame," Babu bragged.

Photographs of Babu and Neema were sent to his studio in the town hall.

Babu's father had written, "You may use these photographs for carving the face of the nymph, but do not use any other part of my daughter-in-law." The photographs were gaudy and showed Neema with her head bowed, her body completely draped but for the shoulders.

Sheshadri knew that Neema visited his wife at the house, but she chose to come when he was away. The town council had come up with a deadline for the carvings. In his nightmares, where demons roared, it was Neema as an apparition that recalled him back to sanity.

Dakshi surprised him one morning with a picture of Neema, a close-up of her face that was uncluttered with gimmickry.

"All I can say is that I'm on your side," she said.

Dakshi had grown thinner, and in the morning mist, her cotton sari clung to her body in graceful curves. Sheshadri had not seen her this clearly before.

He could have her pose for him and use Neema's photograph for the nymph's face. It would be much simpler. But he did not have the courage to compromise with Dakshi and explain to her his infatuation with Neema's face. He asked his mother to have Dakshi visit him in his studio on a predetermined day.

Several months had passed since Neema's marriage, and Babu had fallen back to his old habits. It was the month of November, and the Dassara celebrations in the old kingdom of Mysore had begun. Babu and his friends had virtually camped in a hotel in Mysore City for the duration of the horse races. Nanjangud was deserted. It was raining when Sheshadri left for his studio. Tonight, in the city, the palace of the old king would be lit for the last time. At the Chamundi temple, there would be the celebration of the goddess in praise of her triumph over the demon, Mahishasura. He had asked Dakshi to wear a particular sari. When he heard the hesitant knock on his door, he knew it was she. He busied himself with the newspaper.

"Come in!"

He heard her footsteps and the silver bangles as she closed the door after her. She closed the door sharply, which surprised him, for Dakshi moved in the house like a shadow afraid to cross his path.

"I'm here!" she said.

Sheshadri quickly looked up. It was not Dakshi but Neema in Dakshi's sari and blouse.

"I owe you more than my face," she said as she swiftly unbuttoned her blouse.

The rain outside had turned heavy. Drops pelted the high windowpane with the soft rhythm of a chisel chipping into marble as he made love to his nymph. Neema's photographs lay on the floor. The one Dakshi had given him caught stray drops of rain and stirred. He saw the damp spots spread slowly, unevenly, until the sides of the photograph curled, and her face closed in on itself.

The Lady Chieftain

When I was nine and my brother five, one of our recurring dreads was the arrival of bullock carts full of village women who accompanied their litigant husbands into town and camped in our garden. My father was their trusted lawyer.

Our house in Nanjangud was made of mud walls when my father bought it. I remember the huge queen termite that reigned in the cracks. Her soldiers constantly scrimmaged in the straw that held the mud bricks and spewed mud in ecstasy on our food and in our eyes, until at last my father took the walls down. Termites raged through the clumps of their fortress as the queen—fat, ridged, and yellow—contentedly wriggled in her secure mud groove. My mother, being superstitious, asked for her to be taken elsewhere. The workers took care of the queen when my mother wasn't looking.

Once the walls were restored, my mother renewed her religious festivities, hanging new portraits of gods and goddesses that she garlanded and worshipped daily. Many of her friends sang with her in front of the portraits, and almost every day there was a ceremony. My father wasn't much of a believer, so he attended to the land. By the time I was thirteen, we had an orchard of fruit trees. He made little pathways that crisscrossed around the orchard. One led from the main house to his office. Others meandered through flower bushes or led to the cow shed and the vegetable patch. Beyond this tamed softness, the high grove of eucalyptus, elm, jackfruit, and mango, pruned from their past wilderness, flourished. My mother disliked winding paths and thought they were unsightly, not to mention what forbidden or awful things she might step in while walking through them. My brother and I shared a room adjacent to the new brick wall overlooking an almond-shaped circle. A circus could've pitched its tent in the space. At the center, a giant Burma palm swayed like a tranquil phoenix. On stormy nights, I dreamed that it swished in great arcs.

The village chieftains took over this almond-shaped circle when they arrived to camp in our yard with their bullock carts. When we left for school, the circle would be empty, but when we came back, the place would be bristling with activity. Women in bright, ankle-length skirts scurried around as others mixed spices or tended to fires. Underneath the parked bullock carts, quilts and lanterns supplied cushion, warmth, and light. We hurried through our dinner so we could spy on the tribe or spot faces of

known chieftains and their wives, some of whom
numbered two or three. The senior wives were always
there, but the younger faces changed, depending
upon the chieftains.

We were forbidden by our mother to spy or to ask
important questions. "They're wild and uncivilized,"
she'd say. My father would chuckle. At dusk, taking
turns on each other's shoulders, my brother and I
spied.

The tribes always ate around the blazing fires, their
women moving from one chieftain to another, chat-
tering in exotic dialects. Their ankle bells jangled as
they turned or balanced a plate, and their elbows
glimmered with innumerable bangles. Surely they
danced later, for twirling skirts entered my dreams.
The senior wives sat smoking cheroots, keeping an
eye on the younger wives or giving quick instructions.
After dinner, the wives secured the area while the
chieftains buckled their daggers and walked around
the dark orchard. We could hear voices and sometimes the whack of a dagger on a tree, followed by
bird cries. My brother and I took turns holding each
other up to spy for as long as we could.

One evening a new group came, led by a woman.
She was accompanied by younger women, but we saw
no men other than the drivers of the bullock carts. She
was very tall, with silver streaks of hair playing on her
bony, angular forehead. Her eyes were blue with quick,
dark eyelashes. When she smiled, her cheeks filled up
and she looked very friendly. The silver sari she wore
was tied tightly around her body. Later, she changed

her sari to a skirt, and when she stooped over a cooking fire, I saw her breasts and the diamond rings in her
nose and ears. The second night, she spotted me watching her tie bells on her ankles. Next day, we spied on
her in our father's offices. My father had closed the
doors, so all we could hear was the murmur of talk. My
father always spoke to his clients in an impersonal
manner, but this time we could hardly hear what he
said to her. But I distinctly heard her ankle bells. When
we looked for our mother, she was deep into some puja
and yelled at us not to enter the hall but to pick up our
food in the back veranda where she had left it. We
nicknamed the tribal woman The Wicked Lady.

The tribe's indifference and the absence of men
made us venture out one afternoon while they sat
around the palm tree, chewing tobacco. The Wicked
Lady held a bunch of grapes and beckoned to us.
Encouraged by the younger women, I reached out,
and The Wicked Lady clutched my hand and drew
me close to her. Before I knew, she had her hand
under my knickers. I yelled for my brother, who was
in the same predicament under another lady's hand.
The Wicked Lady was laughing and saying something to her tribe.

"Stop! You're pulling my thing off!" I said, letting go
of the grapes.

Beside me, my brother was yelling shamelessly
about his government being snatched away.

The male guards stood by the bullocks, smiling.
Suddenly, The Wicked Lady planted a robust kiss on
my lips and let me go.

"Take good care of your governments, or I'll steal them!" she yelled. We locked ourselves in our room to assess the damage.

"It hasn't come apart," my brother said, turning his penis around. "I thought she had snapped it!"

I examined myself the same way. My mother never discussed sexual matters, and I never thought that strange women could be so bold and uninhibited. Perhaps my mother was right; they were wild, but I had liked the sensation.

"Are you going to tell mother?" I asked my brother.

"Not if you don't," he said, smiling. This was our first pact. That night the women sang and danced for a long time. Next morning, on our windowsill there were bunches of grapes.

Like pups whose tails were bitten, we watched our moves. We ran quickly by the camp. If The Wicked Lady spotted us, she threw kisses or pressed knuckles against her forehead like a forlorn lover. But as her court trial progressed, she grew uninterested in us and sat under the palm tree reading stacks of documents, continuously smoking cheroots. If she saw us, she'd smile vacuously as if she had forgotten all her naughty mischief. I examined my penis to make sure it was still attractive and even thought of wandering close to her, but my brother wouldn't go along.

"Like a crocodile, she's waiting for the right moment. See the leather satchel she carries? I bet it's full of young governments. I want to keep mine where it is!" he said.

We woke up one morning and she was gone. I caught hold of my father's court clerk.

"Do you know where she went?" I asked innocently enough.

"Why? You're too young to be thinking of women. I'll tell your mother. She'll have you castrated," laughed the crafty buzzard, smelling of bad breath, snuff, and red ink.

Other tribes came and camped.

"What happened to the lady chieftain?" I asked my mother.

"The woman is a mishap, part of this, part of that. Some say part thief, part Australian," she explained.

"She wears diamonds in her nose and ears," I volunteered.

"Yes, I've seen them, too," joined my brother. "Big as Kohinoors. Must've stolen them from Kimberley! Diamonds are forever!" he piped, trying to impress my mother with his geography.

"Kimberley mines are in South Africa, stupid," I said.

"She must be part of that, too, that heathen!" sighed my mother.

I couldn't take it any longer.

"She's not a thief, she's a chieftain and a lady chieftain at that! I wish others had her grace!" I shouted.

My father possessed a straight back that made people comment on how gracefully he walked. Some were already saying I had his gait. After the new wall had been built, my mother had gained weight with all those sweets she and her entourage ate by their gods.

Under the palm tree, I had discovered a small bottle of perfume. I was certain it belonged to The Wicked Lady. Now, I felt as if I couldn't ask my mother what I should do with it.

"You should never associate with wild characters. Who knows what she has done to our name? I'll ask the priest," she was saying as I barged out.

That night, I asked my father about the perfume bottle.

My mother stared.

"Why are you so anxious? What's she to you, anyway?" she interrupted, and began to cry. My father tried to console her, but she ran into the bedroom and locked the door.

What did The Wicked Lady do to my mother? I knew father and mother talked after her first visit. Ever since, my mother had been snapping at us. My little brother knew how to exploit the situation by hanging around and pretending to be sympathetic. He said that mother saw The Wicked Lady with our father.

"Father was kissing The Wicked Lady's scar!"

"A scar? Where?" I hadn't seen one.

"In her belly," he giggled. "I told mother!"

"You're growing into a snitch. What else did you tell mother?"

He wouldn't say. Since The Wicked Lady had left, my mother had filled the washroom with Dettol bottles.

Days later, pretending the question was homework, I asked my mother, "Is there a disease called belly scar?"

She stared at me for a moment, then slapped me in the face. Then she ran into the washroom and began scrubbing her hands.

For the next three days, many religious women came to our house, and the gods on our walls had a field day. My brother joined my mother, mostly because he loved sweets. My father slept in his office, playing records or reading poetry. One afternoon, I was still at school when my brother came after me.

"The Wicked Lady is back," he said. "She gave me a present." In his hand he held a long, beautiful peacock feather.

"Perhaps she'll give you one if you kiss her belly," he joked, midget that he was, holding the feather over his penis.

I hit him and he ran shouting that he'd tell our mother all our secrets. At our house, The Wicked Lady was not alone. There was a man in a red turban and handlebar mustache, smoking the hookah. Over a white tunic, he wore a yellow cummerbund with an encrusted dagger. Their servants moved about slowly, as if they were not enjoying this return. When the man got up to stretch, I saw that he was stooped with an ugly hump on his left shoulder.

I climbed the high window on my own and watched. After dinner, The Wicked Lady and the turbaned man entered their makeshift room under the bullock cart, closing the curtains. The lanterns inside glowed, and the crickets on the palm chirped until I fell desolately asleep in my perch.

On Sunday, the camp was deserted, although the bullock carts were still there. Bullocks sat scratching themselves with their horns and jangling their neck bells.

"They must've gone into town. Let's check their hideout," said my brother.

We pried open the curtains around the cart. It was hard to see everything. The checkered quilts and the embroidered pillows were in disarray. One pillow held the impression of a head. Behind the pillows, the Lady's satchel sagged over a bundle of documents. I quickly looked in. There were many little things that women carry, but I saw no detached and shriveled penises. I thought I saw a dagger under the quilt just as my brother yelled that The Wicked Lady and man were returning. I placed the perfume bottle in her satchel and ran.

"The lady chieftain is going to be married." My mother addressed her announcement specially to me.

"He looks suspicious," I whimpered.

"He's a frontier chief. I'm glad for her." My mother showed me the basket of fruits they had given her. Her mood had changed.

"You've acted strange ever since she came here," she said, offering me an orange. Then she added, "She carries an impure baby."

"Whose impure baby?"

"Anything without religion is impure," she went on. "I scrubbed your brother's hands with Dettol and threw away the peacock feather. I'm sure those wild birds eat worms, insects, even refuse. Just because our

God Muruga rode a sacred peacock, all peacocks aren't clean birds."

We were reading *Romeo and Juliet* at school. "Is love impure? Shakespeare doesn't think so!"

"Shakespeare, your father, you! You've all been spoiled," she wailed as if in a trance, and walked off to one of her gods. Her eyes closed and forthwith a sad devotional song emerged from her lips. She was my mother, but devotional or not, she was a bad singer. I had never thought of The Wicked Lady as someone with a baby, impure or not. Did she grab me because I was a baby?

At school, my grades dropped. I stayed around with seniors after hours, smoked, read dirty books and some Omar Khayyam. One day while I dozed in the back row, the English teacher asked me to define treachery.

"Treachery is a Wicked Lady singing in the wilderness, but that wilderness is paradise enow," I answered as my friends laughed.

The night before The Wicked Lady and her suitor left, I heard my father and mother arguing in the bedroom. My father answered questions calmly, but my mother was hysterical. Under the Burma palm, the fires were out and the bullocks dozed. Nothing moved inside the cart or in the orchard.

Next morning, my father made me take a wedding gift to The Wicked Lady. When I stood close to her, she tousled my hair.

My mother wasn't anywhere when my father came to bid them good-bye. I thought The Wicked Lady blushed when he held her. I waited eagerly for my father to kiss her like in the movies; instead he shook her hand. The Wicked Lady quickly climbed into her cart, and she and her suitor rode almost to the gate of the orchard before the cart stopped. "Here," she called after me, opening the back curtain. I ran so fast I thought that if I flapped my arms I'd fly to her. What was I to say to her? Before I could open my mouth, she showered my head with a wild array of peacock feathers. The feathers stuck to me everywhere, in my hair, over my chest, over my wrists.

"I want you to be a bird of paradise," she said, giving me back the perfume bottle. "Give this to your own lover," she smiled, then whispered, "I carry you," wistfully pointing to her belly.

"Thank our gods and goddesses, no one will steal anything from my body anymore," said my brother at dinner.

My mother said she was going on a pilgrimage. The hotel would send us our meals. My father took me to his office and asked all sorts of questions about school, my friends, and my health. Finally, he asked, "Do you love me?"

"Yes," I said, averting my face.

"I'm glad," he said, and hugged me. I must've imagined a whiff of The Lady's perfume on his cheek.

I decked my pillow with her feathers and stuck several around the high window. I wished for dreams where my father was a red turbaned chief camped in the yard, and The Wicked Lady danced for him in a quilted skirt. They drank jugs of wine and smoked cheroots while peacocks roamed around the Burma palm, glittering with diamonds.

Jamal the Constable

I tell you, attaining your heart's desire and ambition in public service is no easy thing. I started as apprentice constable to the town magistrate, even though my father, Jamal the Elder, retired as daffedar after serving the government for thirty years as if it was his own father. Every man, beast, and insect within a radius of a hundred miles of Nanjangud has shivered at the mention of his name. When he left for the station in the morning—dressed in his khaki, his belt buckle waxed to catch the sun and glint it in the eye of any suspicious character, blinding him instantly from his nefarious plans, his mustache trimmed and curved with vaseline to the position of half-moons on either cheek, his turban around his head frilled an inch taller than that of the Maharaja himself—the whole town beamed with security and contentment. Pedestrians walked from the middle of the road to its side in respect of the Daffedar Sahib. He rode his bicycle as though it was the royal elephant itself that swaggered toward the constabulary with pomp and majesty. He yielded not an inch of the middle of the road to any tonga or bullock cart that crossed his path of law and order. Such were the days of his glory, and even now people gather around to reminisce about Jamal the Elder, Daffedar of Daffedars.

If I were not the son of such a splendid father of such splendid heredity, I'd not have been as patient and understanding of the way in which I have been appointed at such a low level of climbing. I would not have kept my mouth shut at such indifference to my ancestry. After all, the son of a famous father deserves a better rung on the ladder of law than some Brahmin candidate who has passed his intermediate examination with chemistry, botany, and zoology. No doubt these Brahmin boys are very smart with books and pass their examinations with flying colors. But, eating vegetables as they do, I don't think they have the muscle power to chase after a running thief or wrestle body to body with the skinniest murderer. It's only non-Brahmins like myself who, by the grace of the Prophet and the good meat from Sabu's meat shop, have developed the real strength and stamina required in a government job like the police. I also know that if my father were alive and the superior officers he knew all his life were still posted at Nanjangud, he could have simply dropped a hint about his son and I would have been promoted instantly. He is gone, and new faces occupy all the important chairs, but I am certain that good deeds in the service of our government will eventually pay their reward. I am settled in my mind that it will not be long before my antecedents and ability merit what they deserve.

I really do not mind my morning duty, which is to stand guard at the Magistrate's wicket-gate. I am rather proud of being able to show off my new uniform in that capacity. I wear my father's belt buckle, which still catches the sun, and I have trimmed his turban to the size of my head. I've been told that people whisper how much I remind them of my father, though I do not ride a bicycle. I fall into patriotic daydreams, especially on hot mornings. I imagine the Magistrate's house is the government's gold reserve and I its sole guardian. I question anyone who comes five feet near the Magistrate's gate with the authority and curtness of an army captain. My hands are ever ready to reach the stick that hangs at my side. Other times, I imagine that relatives of a thief or murderer are after Your Honor's life and are lurking in shadows for the fraction of that second I slacken so they can rush into the house and take his life away before he has tried their case. But usually no one comes to see the Magistrate at his house. Only some straggling cow, or the washerman's donkey sniffs around the compound and gives me a look or two. I whack them a bit, and they go away. My father used to tell me, "To succeed in the police profession, one has to be as alert and obedient guarding a wicket-gate as guarding the Maharaja's own body and soul."

Your Honor the Magistrate is a good fellow. Though he is a Brahmin vegetarian, he is built like an ox. Meat shop Sabu and the hardware merchant Puttasamy say he is one of the smartest in the head that has ever been posted to Nanjangud. He has been quite amicable toward me. I arrive at the house at 7:00 A.M., stand guard at the wicket-gate till 10:00 A.M. At 10:05, I go in and pick up all the law books and case files Your Honor will have grouped together on the table and wait for him to emerge from the kitchen. I give him a stiff salute, wait for him to dress with the black gown and hood of justice, then follow him to the court chambers, three and a half feet behind as custom requires. At the court, I open the door to his chambers and stand to attention as he goes in. Then I dump all the books in front of the head munshi and wait outside the door within earshot of the munshi. When the Magistrate sits on the bench at 11:00 A.M., I announce that the court is in session. Thereafter, I don't have to worry. I spend the rest of the afternoon chatting with the villagers and the relatives of the accused. They usually invite me over to the court canteen. Though it is a vegetarian place, I eat enough to fill my stomach for the afternoon. The Magistrate rises for the day around 4:00 or 4:30. I collect all the case files and books he wants to be taken back and walk behind him to the house. At the house, I wait for a few minutes to see if the Lady Magistrate wants me to run an errand or two for her. Then I am free.

It is not a bad life. They do not work me hard. Only on rare occasions does the Magistrate fall into a temper. It is on days when he is furious at some lawyer or some knotty problem he cannot solve that he takes it out on me. Once he had this famous lawyer, Mr. Chetty from Mysore City, come to argue a theft case. I don't really know what point the argument was about, but from the manner in which the Magistrate and Mr. Chetty were shouting at each other in English, which is the court language, I was sure it had inflamed the Magistrate's temper quite a bit. The Magistrate did not adjourn the hearing for coffee break as usual, but continued the case until the close of day, keeping everyone hungry. There is no terror like that of a vegetarian Magistrate who has missed his pakodas and coffee break. When he rose for the day, he walked home with a furious pace. I walked, or rather trotted, behind. He was muttering and grumbling in English all the way because he did not want me to understand the unmentionables. He got very mad at my place and shouted that I walked like an arthritic snail and I was the laziest apprentice he had ever had. When we arrived at the house, he remembered the umbrella he had left at the court and swore it was my fault. I knew his moods, so I didn't question his opinion. I simply turned my feet back to the courthouse to retrieve the umbrella before all hell broke loose. It is not a big thing or a chore of impossible proportions to walk back a couple of miles for an umbrella unless, as you are doing so, it starts raining cats and dogs. But I cheered myself that on the way back I wouldn't be drenched. When I returned, the Magistrate's temper was still boiling. He was hysterical that I had used the umbrella to save my subordinate head and wanted to fire me for contempt of court. But the Lady Magistrate intervened with a hot cup of coffee for Your Honor and saved the day for me.

Well, it has been ten months since I began my apprenticeship. The day before yesterday, Lady Magistrate went to Mysore City with her two children to visit her parents. I have been bringing Your Honor meals from the bus stand hotel, in a special tiffin carrier. Before she left, Lady Magistrate said to me, "Jamal, ask the bus stand hotel manager to send the meals for your Sahib with his Brahmin mali. Tell him to wash the carrier twice in hot water and use banana leaf inside."

Well I told the manager the lady's wish, but he said, "Look, Constable Jamal, do you think all my malis are Brahmins? Besides, I'm already short of servers, and if I keep sending my Brahmin mali on delivery service, who is going to tend my kitchen? I tell you, since the lady is gone, it doesn't matter. I'll put the tiffin carrier in a gunny bag so you can carry it without touching."

Yesterday, I brought the meals for the Magistrate and left them on his table. He didn't ask me any questions as to who might have touched them. I think he is a liberal man when his wife is away and doesn't bother his legal head with Brahmin/Muslim caste-business that women are so concerned about.

But today, when I brought his lunch, he told me not to go for the evening meal but to wait at the gate, as he was expecting a guest. This was unusual, as the Magistrate usually dismissed me after I walked him home. Also, this was Friday, my night to get together with Sabu and Puttasamy at Bayamma's den to smoke ghanja and drink toddy.

I stood at the wicket-gate, cursing my fate. Around 7:30, I heard the motorcycle of the assistant superinten-dent of police puttering toward the house. I got up from my guard bench and straightened my uniform. I saluted the A.S.P. stiffly and promptly as he cut the engine. He asked me if the Magistrate was in the house and ordered me to take the cycle to the back of the house and park it there. He was inside the house for about half an hour, then he came out with Your Honor. They were laughing and talking in English in a pleas-ant out-of-the-office sort of manner. The Magistrate, as he passed me, said, "Jamal, I want you to stay at the house all evening, as I hear a lot of burglary is going on. Keep the thermos with you for my morning coffee."

I said, "Yes, Your Honor." in a meek voice. They walked slowly toward the Traveler's Bungalow, which is beyond the courthouse. I cursed my fate again. No ghanja or toddy for me tonight. I didn't have the slight-est warning of this special duty. If I had known, I'd have sent words to Sabu about it. Probably they were already at Bayamma's den waiting for me. Perhaps Bayamma had made one of her special lamb kurma for us and kept the toddy cool in her earthen pot. My mouth began to water and my body yearned for those heavenly blue puffs of ghanja. But I am a good Muslim. I make namaz twice regularly and practice my faith. Maybe Allah will understand my conflict between my public and my private selves and do some-thing. My father used to say, "Jamal, your private self should obey your public self. That is the beauty of ser-vice. It will bring you many benefits and many joys that eventually you can enjoy as a private self." I am not sure that my father, when he said that, was referring to my present dilemma, which as a non-ghanja smoker he could not have guessed.

Allah must have somehow heard my prayers, for I saw Sabu and Puttasamy walking towards the house. My heart leaped with delight as they came near. "I greet you, my friends," I said. "Only the goodness of your combined hearts must have brought you here!"

Sabu came closer and whispered, "No, dear friend. Bayamma kicked us out for not paying for services the last time we used her den. She said, 'Police protection or no police protection, either pay for my services or find another who can do it as well as I do, I challenge you!' So, since you didn't appear, we thought we should come to you and see what you'd suggest!"

We went to the back of the house where there is a small room that was once used as a storeroom for firewood. It has been empty since the Lady Magistrate bought a Primus stove and fixed a water heater in the bathroom. It was not comparable to Bayamma's den, which was furnished with pillows and soft coir mats, but there was an old quilt and a tarnished wicker lamp that still worked. Puttasamy opened his bulging gunny bag and took out three toddy bottles. Then he unwrapped the ghanja from a dry banana leaf. I could smell that it was the very best. Puttasamy had used his slow mind to stop at the bus stand hotel and had brought some pakodas and ompudi for us to munch with.

We settled down to our feast. It was good toddy and good ghanja. Time went flying, as our Urdu poet

Omar has said. The sweet slow smoke of ghanja filled my lungs with buoyancy and serenity. My aching calf muscles relaxed, and I felt strong and afraid of nothing. Companionship of masculine friends is one of the pleasures that men share without even speaking a word. But ghanja and toddy are not items that induce silent enjoyment. They loosen the tongue and make the spirit fly freely. My friends gossiped a while about town matters. Then they began inquiring about my master and family. I told them of the Lady Magistrate's visit and the bringing of meals from the bus stand. It was then that Sabu asked, "Why do you think your sahib did not eat a vegetarian meal tonight?" I had not thought of that seriously until then. These Brahmins have crazy eating habits. Sometimes they eat a lot at one sitting and somtimes they starve themselves to death in the name of some auspicious occasion—unlike us Muslims, who starve only during Ramadan.

"How would I know?" I replied. "Maybe he doesn't like hotel meals, maybe he misses his wife's cooking or maybe he misses his children. Why should it matter so much?" The ghanja was having a heavenly effect on me. I wanted these friends to realize that I had guts and that I was not a meek constable. My heart and spirit were those of a Daffedar. I wanted them to ask me more about myself instead of wasting our good times with a lot of gossip about higher authorities. But Sabu went on like he had not heard me.

"I have heard of the sahib's fondness for nonvegetarian meals!" he said.

I was shaken. This was not an irresponsible matter to gossip. I am a servant of the government, and the Magistrate was the immediate incarnation of the government I served. "Government's work is God's work," my father used to say, and I am no traitor, high on ghanja or not.

"What is this you say?" I retorted with some anger. "I have been serving Your Honor for ten months and perhaps I know him better than even his wife does! I carry his files and listen to his judgments. I hear him and see him all the time except when he is sleeping. I have never seen him eat meat. Why should he? He's built like an ox vegetarianly. He likes his radish sambar and pickles. Why throw gutter water on the character of a high-caste officer? You had better stop talking like that."

Puttasamy, who until then was silently smoking, added, "Jamal, don't be blind with patriotism. I have heard such rumors, too. What is more, yesterday Sabu supplied Joseph of the Traveler's Bungalow with prime cuts of lamb and one whole Australian leghorn hen that he had to specially order from the Mysore Russell Market. But Joseph is not having any visitor in the Traveler's Bungalow! Today I saw Joseph's wife in the market buying all sorts of vegetables and spice. Do you think she has gone rich overnight, or become pregnant in her fifty-fifth year? The A.S.P. is a non-vegetarian, and it seems your Magistrate and he were good friends before they were posted here!" He paused and then added, "Don't think that is all that's happening in the Traveler's Bungalow tonight!"

I did not know what he meant or whether I heard him right. I took some deep gulps of toddy and pulled swiftly on the ghanja to suppress my shock. Why should these two intimate friends of mine lie about such things? They had no grudge against the Magistrate or the A.S.P. Besides, they had enough trouble smoking and drinking without being caught or exposed to their families. Still, I was not thoroughly convinced. My father used to say, "Everyone wants to see through a policeman's eye because that will make their own evidence acceptable. But as a policeman, don't be fooled by the sight of others. See for yourself everything as well as the Prophet would permit before you make evidence." I wanted to go see for myself, but I did not want my friends to think that I believed their story.

It was about the hour of midnight. Sabu and Puttasamy were now well smoked, fed, and drunk. I suggested that we call it a night and disband before the neighbors got suspicious of the lamp in the old firewood room. They agreed. I walked with them to the gate of the house and bid them good-bye. I waited until I could no longer see them beyond the streetlight corner. Then, steadying my stumble as best as I could, I walked toward the Traveler's Bungalow.

The streets were dark and empty. In the dustbins I could hear stray dogs turning over the banana leaves the housewives had thrown out after the evening meal. The stars were shining like they were wiped clean after a wash. The night breeze felt delicious on my body. As I approached the bungalow, my suspicions grew. The

main room, which is always reserved for visiting dignitaries, had its light on. I could see both ceiling fans
whirring through the ventilators. I went closer until I
was under the gul mohr tree in front of the bungalow.
Its branches, which extended over the roof of the patio,
were full of summer flowering. There were many crickets chirping away the cool night in the branches. *Happy
rascals*, I thought. *How free and irresponsible are they.
They eat and drink free from mother nature and whistle all
night like vagabonds. But then they do not know the pleasure of ghanja or the satisfaction that results from being a
police officer.* My thoughts were interrupted by the
opening of the main-room door. Joseph the butler
emerged with a tray of plates. I ducked under a bush.
He emptied the plates of the leftovers. As he emptied
them, I could see pieces of chewed chicken bones, slices
of beets and cucumber.

The rich aroma of rice biryani floated over to my
nostrils. Joseph went back into the room and returned
with two bottles. My heart began to pound faster.
Though my vision was blurry, I could make out the
fact that they were foreign whiskey bottles. He set
them on the floor next to the kitchen door where he
had already set several empty soda bottles. As he came
out of the main room, he had left the door ajar and I
could hear male and female voices. Then a woman
came out. I had never seen her before. She was dressed
in a blue silk sari and wore many silver bangles. Her
face, though a little fat in the cheek, was soft and per-
fumed. I could smell the faint fragrance of Hazeline
Snow. Her lips were juicy with the chewing of betel,

and she kept steadying her sari over her shoulder. As she did so, I could see she was grandly endowed with pleasures of flesh a man always dreams of.

Joseph came running from the kitchen. She said to him, "The judge sahib wants some coffee in an hour. Bring some fresh soda for now!" Joseph withdrew. The beautiful woman stood at the door, making bangle noises. Hot beads of perspiration trickled down my crouching armpits with the consistency of rivulets. Could she be the paramour of Your Honor! Could Your Honor be a meat-eater, a drinker of foreign whiskey, a lover of exotic women? I crouched lower, as though burdened by such confusing thoughts. My head reeled more now as the full effect of the night's indulgence was taking over.

Then someone came out of the room and encircled the woman's waist with an oxlike reach. His embracing hand wandered all over her. He kept reaching for her mouth, which was somewhat difficult from his side position, and he ended up landing kisses on her cheek. His shirt hung outside his pants and a button on his fly was peeping.

I blushed visibly. I could not see clearly, nor did I want to. The oxlike frame of the man was enough to make me withdraw. What was I to do? I am a public servant, sworn to uphold the integrity of the country, but no one, not even my father, had told me what to do or say if and when I saw a judge in such a condition! As I returned to the house, deep feelings of guilt possessed me. I even entertained my floating mind to convince itself that it could not be Your Honor that I had seen.

I could not think or worry anymore. Mercifully, the ghanja was calling all my organs to sleep. I left all my responsibilities in the trust of the Almighty to sort out my confusion somehow while I slept.

The next morning, I had the feeling that the previous evening was just a nightmare. I could barely recollect the events in any order. Outside, the sun was already high. I realized with a start that I had to bring Your Honor's morning coffee. I rushed to the hotel and when I came back with it, the Magistrate was sitting in the hall with the a.s.p. Someone had already brought them breakfast and coffee. I saluted my master, but he simply glared at me. The town hall gong struck eleven. I had overslept!

Two weeks later, at the end of a regular court day, I went to pick up the case files when the Magistrate called me to his chambers. He said, "Jamal, I have good news for you! You've now worked under me for almost a year. You've been a good apprentice police constable. I've therefore decided to transfer you to Gundlupet with a promotion that you be appointed constable with honors."

My heart opened and shut like the swing door on Your Honor's chambers. The Magistrate was saying the words that I had always dreamt of! To be promoted to full-time constable before the termination of apprenticeship, with personal recommendation of the Magistrate, was indeed very good news. After the bungalow incident, all I had feared was the discovery of my spying and dismissal from service! The Magistrate continued cutting short my brain's activity.

"Now, Jamal, there's one important thing that I want to impress upon you. It's important for your future prospects that you exercise restraint in your nocturnal habits. Yes, I've come to know you are a heavy smoker of ghanja, and the heavy smoking has resulted in what we in the legal profession call hallucination. It is a common phenomenon among users, and I have here on my shelves volumes of case law from England and the Supreme Court of India, citing such phenomena." He paused to catch his breath, then continued. "In the case of master and servant, they usually have to do with the suppressed hostility of the servant for the master, and psychologists explain that this usually results in sensual fabrication in the servant's mind about his master's private life. The servant, under the influence of the drug of such smoke, comes to believe in these fabrications to the extent of actually being convinced that he has witnessed any event that the servant wishes to involve his master in. Now, I know you're a good man, and you're sound of mind and body. Therefore, I advise you that, if you've been experiencing any such phenomena during your apprenticeship, you should forthwith cease from smoking ghanja, at least until you're well settled in Gundlupet, and thereafter use restraint when you have to indulge in such habits." He smiled benignly.

I was speechless. How in the world did he find out about my spying? Is it possible that what I believe I actually saw was not what actually happened? Your Honor looked so virtuous as he spoke to me in his gown and hood. He was such a smart man, so full of law and precedent. One could not become Magistrate simply by being a Brahmin. One had to be born with the virtue of it. Why should he be so benevolent toward me unless what he had found out in the books is true and I was indeed suffering hallucinations? I smoked so much ghanja I could not be sure which days I was hallucinating and which days I was not. If he was seeking revenge, then why did he promote me instead of firing me? It did not follow, as I have heard lawyers say while arguing their cases. Your Honor was well-founded and compassionate. If the fat books of law said it was hallucination, who was I to question their credibility? Ignorance of law was no excuse, even if the law was in English.

In gratitude, I prostrated to my full length and touched the shoes of Your Honor. Then I went to tell the good news to the Lady Magistrate. She was happy for me. She said I would do well in Gundlupet. Then she paused for a second and asked, "Tell me, Jamal, when I was away, did you hear of any function in the Traveler's Bungalow?" I shivered, but I used my presence of mind and said I had not. She looked at me strangely, as women do when they cannot figure out what you are thinking.

The next day a mark appeared on the Magistrate's forehead that was green in the beginning, then turned to all kinds of colors, and eventually shot out like a horn. This only increased his reputation. The clerks in the court were saying the Magistrate had hit his head on the corner of his bookshelf late in the night as he reached for a hefty book. But the horn looked more like someone had put it there. I did not want to think too much about it and fall into one of those hallucinations.

Next morning, I went to the back door of the house to pay my respects to the Lady Magistrate. She stood beside the kitchen door as though she didn't want to be seen fully. She gave me the umbrella of Your Honor as a parting gift. Your Honor was sleeping. Why should a Magistrate get up to bid good-bye to a constable! I picked up my belongings and walked to the bus stand.

The bus to Gundlupet departed in the evening instead of the afternoon, for it had developed punctures in all the rear wheels and the conductor had to wait for another bus to arrive with the jack. As the bus left town, I could not help a feeling of sad warmth. In the yellow light, the houses of the town looked like they were in a fairy tale. We passed by the market, the police station, and the Magistrate's house. The wicket-gate looked desolate without my standing on guard. I imagined how I must have appeared to a passerby or a passenger on a bus. The last building we passed by was the Traveler's Bungalow, which at this time of the evening was empty except for two cows that sat on the patio, munching. Joseph must have gone to the market. Some boys sat on the gul mohr tree, and the branches were shaking with their exuberance; the ground under was covered with red flowers of gul. Everything about Nanjangud looked harmonious and pleasant. Even the dust the bus churned up gave the road a hazy dignity.

I fell into a delirious nap helped by the trundling
rhythm of the bus and the monotony of villagers'
chatter. Some hours must have passed. I was suddenly woken by a pothole. What I saw in the front
seat jolted my heart around its cavity. The unknown
woman I had seen that night in the bungalow was
sitting there with another lady. The woman was as
beautiful as ever and her expensive silver bangles jangled as well when she moved her arms. I could smell
the familiar fragrance of Hazeline Snow. They must
have got on the bus somewhere along the way.
Where were they going? Where did they come from?
Were they real? Questions floated past my mind in a
torrent. The man next to me jabbed me in the side
and winked meaningfully. He had bad teeth, and
what was left of them was seeped in betel juice. The
unknown woman was not bothered but seemed
amused by his gesture.

In Gundlupet there is also a Traveler's Bungalow.
Once in a while, as I pass by it on my duty, I see
women there who resemble the unknown woman in
their beauty and dress. I give them the benefit of the
doubt. My father used to say, "A shut mouth not only
will not speak but it will make your face memorable
where it matters." When I want to smoke ghanja, I go
to the cycle shop Gowda, who has a shack at the back.
We smoke there in peace, free of provocation, and
afterward I sleep there for the night. My superior
officer is a sub-inspector and a non-Brahmin. He
respects my experience and relies on my legal knowledge on many matters.

It is not a bad life. People of Gundlupet are slowly getting to know me. The bus stand hotel manager invites me to eat anything I want. Nanjangud is a fading memory, a past foothold to the present rung on my ladder. I hear other constables gossip that it will not be long before I am promoted to fill the shoes of my erstwhile father Jamal the Elder, the Daffedar of Daffedars.

The Holy Wristwatch

Even before the famous swamiji arrived in Nanjan-gud, Kalayya had heard of his powers—how, in front of a believer's eye, he could materialize gifts from heaven. Kalayya believed in the spiritual, though when he was a boy, a wandering hermit had taken his mother's silver bangle, promising a gold one. The hermit had wrapped the bangle in a holy cloth and had asked her to open it three days later. When she did, instead of gold, the bangle had turned into glass. Kalayya's mother said it was God's will and wore it proudly for the rest of her life.

But the swamiji from Mysore City was revered across the country. He was camping in Nanjangud on the invitation of the town elders, to bless the new house in the extension that contractor Mohan Velu had built for himself. That evening, the swamiji was giving Darshan to the general public. Mohan Velu had erected a Shamiana, and already a sizable crowd had gathered. Kalayya made his way through the curious until he could stand close enough to the wealthy, who sat cross-legged on the floor in front of the swamiji. The magistrate's wife was singing a religious song while Mohan Velu's wife and daughter were distributing flowers. Then it was time for the gathered to pay homage to the holy one.

The magistrate's son, who had already failed to matriculate three times, touched the swamiji's feet and laid a gift in front of him. Pulling the boy close, the swamiji whispered the holy in his ear. Then the unbelievable happened. Out from nowhere, the swamiji materialized a shining new gold watch, which he swiftly buckled onto the boy's wrist. There was applause and bowing. One by one, the town's sons and daughters formed a column in the center of the gathering and approached the holy man. The swamiji blessed each of them with one miracle after another: an apple for the primary school teacher, a pen and pencil set for lawyer Shankar Chetty's son, a brooch for grocer Puttasamy's daughter.

It was a spectacle Kalayya wished his mother were alive to see. Even on her dying day, she had spoken to Kalayya about her sacred glass bangle. She wished it to be a parting gift to whomever he would marry. Kalayya had kept the bangle safe, and whenever his eyes fell on some gainsome village girl on his way to the Kirloskar construction, he could daydream about how the glass bangle would look upon her wrist. The bangle would also be the test of her true character. If she laughed at his mother, then she would not be the one to share his life.

The last disciple to bring gifts to the swamiji was Mohan Velu's daughter, and once again, to everyone's astonishment, the swamiji materialized another watch. This one sparkled with diamonds. Everyone rose to their feet to chant, "Swamiji-ki-Jai!" With a serene smile, the holy one walked around the inner circle, touching a head here, putting his toothmarks on a lemon there. Then his eyes wandered over to settle on Kalayya, who stood with his hands in suppliance. The swamiji asked him who he was.

"I'm a laborer at the Kiroskar construction," replied a trembling Kalayya.

The swamiji asked him to kneel, then placed his hands over his head.

"In God's eyes, the rich and the poor, the high and the lowly, the good and the bad, all are one," he said, and tied another miraculous watch around Kalayya's wrist. The crowd fell into a hush as the holy one retreated to his quarters inside the contractor's house.

Kalayya became the talk of the town. This was the first time a total stranger had been singled out by the swamiji. "You're a lucky fellow to receive such a valuable gift from such a holy spirit!" commented tailor Ramjin. Watch repairman Hamid examined the watch and said its case was electroplated with silver.

"This may not be as good a watch as the Swiss watches the swamiji materialized, but you're fortunate to get one for nothing!" Hamid said.

Kalayya wondered if the swamiji had divined what had happened to his mother's silver bangle. How else could he have singled him out for such just retribution?

He wore the wristwatch only after he had finished his work and had scrubbed his brick-carrying hands up to the elbows with soap and water. While he worked, he kept the watch safely wrapped in his handkerchief. Fellow coolies at the construction would tease him when he refused to tell them the time. The foreman taunted him.

"Why do you keep a wristwatch when you don't even wear it like a normal owner? I'll give you twenty-five rupees for it."

Kalayya would not part with it. He had found out from Hamid how much the watch would cost. The foreman was offering not even half its price. Besides, what would his mother think! It was not every day a miracle came in the way of a poor laborer.

One Friday when Kalayya wore the watch to go to the cinema, he discovered it had stopped running. Hamid opened up the case. One of the tiny springs was broken. Hamid charged him five rupees to replace it. The watch ran well for a week and then it stopped. Hamid said it needed new screws and another spring.

"You should never trust desi watches like this one. There's always something wrong with our government products. You should've asked for at least a Japanese watch from the swamiji. I serviced the magistrate's son's watch, and it's worth its value in gold bullions!"

It was going to cost him twenty-five rupees, an entire month's salary, to buy the parts. Hamid was an honest and hardworking Muslim. Kalayya had no reason to believe he was being overcharged.

"I'll pay you one rupee every month until I'm out of your debt," he urged Hamid.

"I trust you," Hamid replied. "But I have to buy the spare parts from the city. I make a living day-to-day, just like you. Even after I fix it, I cannot promise it'll run without trouble."

The foreman came to the rescue.

"I hear the swamiji has just come back from America and is holding purification meetings in Mysore City. Why don't you take it back? Maybe he'll give you another one."

Mysore City was fourteen miles away. Kalayya worked overtime and got the foreman's permission to catch the Friday afternoon bus. The bus driver let him ride for half-price. "After all, you're going on a holy mission," he said, and asked him to mention his name to the swamiji.

When Kalayya reached the swamiji's mansion, it was sunset. There were many cars parked in front. A tall bearded man in saffron robes met him at the doorway. It was the swamiji's personal secretary. He listened patiently to Kalayya.

"The holy swamiji is not a magician to give you a new watch for an old one. You'll be foolish to ask the swamiji to take his gift back," he said.

"I only want a watch that ticks. This one has already cost me five rupees to fix, and the repairman says it'll cost me a month's salary for new springs and screws."

The secretary was growing impatient. Well-dressed city worshippers were waiting for his attention.

"Maybe the repairman is playing games with you. How do I know this is the same watch the swamiji gave you!"

Kalayya insisted that he should at least have darshan with the swamiji.

"I've traveled all the way from Nanjangud, and there are no buses that go back tonight. I'll have to sleep outside some temple or in the market. It does not matter if the swamiji cannot fix my watch. I want to pay him my respects and tell him that I've always believed in his powers."

The secretary reluctantly allowed him in. The ceremonies had not yet begun, and the swamiji was sitting in his office behind a large desk conversing with two foreigners. Kalayya bowed to the swamiji and touched his feet.

"Honorable Sir, I'm neither ungrateful nor selfish. When you honored Nanjangud with your visit, you gave me this wristwatch. I'd like to give it back, as I've no use for it."

Kalayya could not help it. How could he insinuate anything wrong about a gift the great swamiji had bestowed on him, in front of such distinguished foreigners? The swamiji did not recognize him. He picked up the watch from where Kalayya had placed it and held it to his ear.

"This is not working. No wonder you wish to give it back!" he said, and laughed. The foreigners joined him. The secretary came in to say it was time. The swamiji gave the watch back.

"I cannot help you with such material tribulations," he said as he rose from the chair. "It's your concern with the watch as a possession and your blindness to its symbolic significance that has caused you all this suffering. You should focus your eye inward on your soul and prevail over material wantings."

Kalayya bowed as the swamiji stopped. He felt the swamiji's hand over his head. When he rose, the swamiji had materialized a packet of sacred ash, which he smeared on Kalayya's forehead. Then, bending over, he quickly whispered, "Sell it!"

Giddy with the encounter, Kalayya walked out of the mansion. He could hear the gathering in the prayer hall chanting, "Swamiji-ki-Jai!" He carefully wrapped the sacred ash along with the wristwatch and walked toward the market.

The Elephant Stop

Seven days before the commencement of the Dassara celebrations in the kingdom of Mysore, on its morning walk through the city, the royal elephant refused to budge beyond the corner where the main bazaar street and the temple of Kali met.

There was no explanation for its behavior. It looked happy and swung its trunk jauntily as always, except it did not wish to move beyond the shade of the gul mohr tree, which, thanks to its chance existence at that very spot, provided enough shade until the matter was looked into. The chief mahout arrived and examined the beast, particularly its legs. He coaxed it with a sack of coconuts. The elephant grabbed as many coconuts as it could, trumpeted its glee, but stayed steadfast. People gathered. The mahout ordered guards and departed in haste. Now, there's nothing unusual about an elephant stopping during its walk anywhere it pleases. They have sturdy legs and sleep while standing. But unlike circus elephants trained to do awkward maneuvers for the titillation of the public, the royal elephant is trained by masters in the art of mammalian etiquette. Its behavior in public is crucial to the dignity and decorum of the royalty. The present elephant's great-grandfather was famous for its impeccable manners; it had expired one day with its head turned to the wall in such a graceful manner that it looked as if it were napping. Rigor mortis set in, and it took a half-dozen mahouts and as many poles to roll the corpse down.

The Dassara celebrations were only days away, and the royal astrologer had predicted that everything would go smoothly. News of the elephant's behavior spread to the palace. The master-in-charge of the Dassara celebrations came to inspect the situation. He was a shrewd man. He did not wish to cause any anxiety to the king before he was certain there was no alternative. He sent for the veterinarian. The veterinarian examined the elephant with a stethoscope and ordered some pills to be given three times daily in sugarcane juice. A chapra was built over the elephant's head with bamboo poles and then thatched with palms. Over the roof, the purple canopy with the royal insignia was hoisted. The elephant's personal sweeper, washer, and manicurist were posted. More guards arrived to secure the area. The elephant stood majestically flapping its ears, swinging its well-groomed tusks this way and that.

Next morning, it became clear that the elephant would not move. Maharaja Chamadharma—King Chum to his British friends at the Race Course Club— sat with a hangover. He had missed the auspicious

Tuesday morning puja to the royal deity and was worried about a possible curse. Perhaps he would slip while playing tennis. King Chum's father, Raja Raja Verma—King Verm to his friends at Buckingham Palace—had neglected rituals so badly that on the first day of his first Dassara, he had tripped on the footstool to the throne and broken his kneecap. He limped somewhat for the rest of his life. Chamadharma sent for the royal astrologer. The queen simply said, "It's my husband's karma catching up! His sordid affairs with English women and whiskey!"

It was common knowledge that the king and the queen did not sleep together. Their marriage was one of politics. She was plump, superstitious, interested in embroidery, nuts, sweets, and gossip. The king had been trained in a school for princes in Paris. They had no issue.

The royal astrologer examined the pachyderm, inquired about the direction of its head when it came to a standstill, and made his calculations. The elephant had stopped because of some spiritual static that must have occurred at the intersection. The Kali temple nearby could be the source. The animal, with its extrasensory perception, must have seen something evil. He would prepare an amulet for the elephant and offer special puja to Goddess Kali.

The elephant did not move.

By the evening of the third day, the elephant stop had become a point of public interest. Women found it a god-sent opportunity to worship. They offered it coconuts, jaggery, and rice, and brought their children for a chance to stomp on its droppings. But the droppings were sacred and were removed by the sweeper before they had a chance—a wagon stood nearby, ready to cart off the containers for burial in the royal grounds. Villagers parked their bullock carts, causing traffic jams. Motorcars and the city bus were detoured to other streets. An enterprising Brahmin saw an opportunity and put up a coffee stand. Hawkers with fruits, vegetables, and flowers appeared. The town newspaper carried headlines with route directions to the elephant stop.

In the palace, there was a steady mounting of panic. Unless the elephant got back to the palace, there was no Dassara. If it were left to Chamadharma, he would have tied it up and brought it back in a lorry. But that would have caused unimaginable chaos in the palace and in the mind of the public. The beast was sacred. It was the incarnation of God Ganesha. No force could be used against its will. Chamadharma had enough trouble keeping his karma within manageable limits.

The astrologer made more calculations and revealed that the problem was more complicated. The entire royalty had to purify themselves. He narrated from an old text that had been written many years before the coming of the Mughals and the British. The then-Maharaja of Mysore had issued a stone edict at the very spot the elephant had stopped. The edict spoke of the king's belief that elephants are the most noble beasts on earth. He had erected a marble statue of the then-royal elephant next to it. The present royal elephant had remembered both the edict and some wrongdoing to itself and had fallen into a trance.

Therefore it was necessary to do the following: first, the king should undertake pilgrimage to the Tirumalai hills. The queen and the courtesans should fast for three days. The palace should offer silver and food to all the Brahmin pujaris of the kingdom. Further, the courtesans should gather at the elephant stop on the fifth day to worship and bathe the animal under the supervision of the royal astrologer.

The king thought the whole thing a farce. An elephant stops and everyone jumps to religious conclusions! What if he celebrated the Dassara without it? What if he substituted another who looked exactly alike? He asked if there were any restrictions on the type of his travel. There were none. He ordered his plane to be prepared. The queen welcomed the purifications. Fasting would be good for her body and mind. She had been eating too many sweets. The courtesans did not like any of it. But they existed through the royal patronage, so they had to do what they were told.

The king left immediately with his personal assistant and dress boy. The royal plane was seen heading in the direction of the hills. The courtesans' march to the elephant stop became the talk of the town. The local newspaper carried stories with pictures on each of the seventeen courtesans. Literary luminaries contributed articles on the event and the role of religion in human conduct. The day the courtesans began their procession, the entire route was jammed with people. The radio supplied running commentary. The procession was a solemn affair, since the courtesans, most of them middle-aged, were weak without food. The most senior of them led the group. She was sixty-five and had to rest under an umbrella every few steps. The royal orchestra accompanied the group with slow, pensive dirges. When the courtesans arrived at the elephant stop, the astrologer instructed the senior courtesan to shave the elephant's navel area and to apply a concoction of herbs. The others went around the beast, touching its trunk, its belly, its tail, chanting forgiveness. People were touched. Finally, the courtesans washed the elephant with jugs of sacred water, pouring it over designated areas of its body to the chanting of the astrologer. The royal orchestra played mournful tunes from Hindi movies, then settled back to their favorite medley from the "follies."

The elephant lifted its trunk and salaamed repeatedly.

The sixth day came. The king returned, looking pale and exhausted. He had pondered over the absurdity of the whole situation en route to the hills and had had the pilot change the course to Bombay. He had spent his time in the Taj Mahal Hotel. The queen lost three pounds. She moved through the palace with the swiftness of an impala, her face beaming with religious virtuosity.

Exactly five hours before the morning of the Dassara, the elephant let out a huge fart and abruptly moved from the elephant stop.

The Reincarnation

Gravity is depressing

When octogenarian Pillai, divine founder and director of Paramayoga Ashram, stood at the rim of the huge wooden drum with his hands in supplication and his eyeballs rolled precariously upward into his eyelids revealing their acrylic white, the crowd that had gathered for the announced miracle fell into hypnotic stillness. Pillai, dressed in the traditional white dhoti, had fasted for three weeks. He was frail by nature and siddhi, though his gait was still that of a man who walked on ground buffeted by a spiritual cushion of air. His feet were shapely, and his insoles displayed a pink softness that defied explanation. Others in the ashram who had yet to attain siddhi had glaringly plain calluses that they had acquired despite wearing sandals. Pillai was unpunctured by man or nature. His three weeks' fast was a necessary prologue to his attempt to walk on water; it was meant to get rid of any unknown impurity in his feet and body that might conflict with his spiritual conquest of gravity. Pillai's disciples swore that they had seen their leader levitate from his coir mat during the last few prayer meetings. It was imperceptible at first—Pillai in meditation before a cluster of incense sticks, levitating to the burnt tip of the sticks before they were out. Last night, he had risen to the burning tip—this was a private meditation to which only his most senior disciples were invited. Word, however, had spread from Nanjangud to all the nearby towns and villages. If the yogic master could levitate from a coir mat, he surely could cradle his feet for the fraction of time that it would take for him to walk across a drum of water.

The wooden drum had been specially made for the occasion and filled with the blessed water from the Indian Ocean, where once Sri Rama had built a bridge to rescue his wife Sita from the demon king Ravana of Sri Lanka. Ponnsamy, the town ironsmith, had built the drum to rigid specifications. It was ten feet high and five feet wide. The planks were cut from a balsam tree that grew in the ashram yard and had been chosen over many others for its eternal greenness and for the angle at which it had grown, shading part of the ashram prayer center. Even the steel plates that held the drum together were sanctified. A wooden ladder was built to allow Pillai to climb to a small platform alongside of which the drum's filled surface waited for Pillai's ethereal steps.

Pillai shut his eyes and offered a silent prayer in preparation. The sight of the frail yogi, whose compassion and charity were well-known in Nanjangud, prompted his admirers to cajole their own favorite gods and goddesses to lend him support. This would be an act of faith. Pillai was not like many others in the country who sold their mystic shakti to the highest bidder or who surrounded themselves with rich Western misfits in showy acts of feigned holiness. Gods must have known that Pillai had shunned such performances. There was not a single Westerner in his ashram, though many had sought his patronage. Pillai had not even visited or accepted any invitations to visit other ashrams and centers. He had dedicated himself to one place, his Paramayoga Ashram. So why shouldn't the gods and goddesses of holy India lend him their support for just a fraction of a second? No one but the believers who had gathered there would know of it. Others would call it a hoax and be left to wallow in their own blindness. Pillai would never do a repeat just to convince those who had no faith. The skeptical world was never welcome in his ashram, nor the world of wealth and temptation.

But this world is such a stubborn and settled place. Pillai opened his eyes, and with his hands joined high above his head in prayer, he stepped onto the dark green ocean in front of him. He placed his right foot in first, as if gingerly testing the elusive surface, then quickly propelled his left over it in a long, wide stride. For the blink of an eye, it appeared as though the master had indeed accomplished the impossible, for Pillai had balanced himself on the spineless back of the deep. But it was only a blink. With the implanting of his left foot, Pillai sank quietly to the bottom, and before the crowd could recover from its dismayed gape, he resurfaced at the rim of the wooden drum, holding onto it for dear life. The divine attendants quickly pulled him to safety. Someone threw a blanket around his body, and he was briskly carried inside the ashram. It was all over before it began, and the worshippers stood spellbound.

No one moved. A boy who had climbed up an ashram tree yelled "He sank like a stone!" Then, one by one, the crowd broke the circular harmony of their gathering, shaking their heads as if it were a bad dream, in ones and twos, erratic and staggering towards no particular destination. Someone said the problem was the choice of hour, which, according to his own calculations, was evil. Others blamed the failure on the impurities that contaminated the mythic ocean, or the spot from which the water had been transported, or all those Western ships of war. Only the Anglo-Indian population of Nanjangud quietly relished Pillai's failure; it had kept their faith intact.

"If only we had concentrated on walking on water before we learned how to fly in aluminum tubes through the air, we would have been the superior country," lamented a disciple.

No one blamed Pillai or felt that he had failed, for the task had been superhuman. Some disciples admired him even more, for after failing to walk on water, he retired into seclusion and vowed he'd not speak again. Citizens of Nanjangud tried to dissuade him; even in a mechanized country like America, rockets and missiles put together by Nobel prize-winners went awry, for heavenly powers always had the last say in such matters. Pillai should try again, at a more auspicious time. Pillai shook his head vehemently and wrote a message to one and all: man was not ready for such feats because the gods didn't trust him. Let man conquer gravity and he would surely wreck the balance of mother earth. The planet would catapult to oblivion. The gods had chosen Pillai's failure as a warning to all mankind that it was they who kept the balance in the universe, not man.

On the seventh day of his seclusion, Pillai fell into a coma. He was transferred to a hospital where, despite all modern medicinal therapies, he failed to regain consciousness. At the luminous hour of midnight of the full moon, Pillai took his last deep breath. According to his wish, he was buried in a squatting position in a cement cubicle with his prayer beads and a copy of the Gita. His disciples added a few items of necessity, such as a new pair of dhoti, a flashlight, dried fruits and nuts. They knew such a yogic master had to return to life, but how and when? A few slept close to the burial for several days just to be sure, their ears primed to hear human thuds from the ground below.

On Pillai's eighty-first birthday, word came that in the town of Gubbi, ninety-three miles from Nanjangud, village women while washing clothes at the town pond had discovered a naked child asleep on a green banana leaf. The nearest banana plantation was a hundred miles away. A cobra, its hood raised, guarded the child. When awakened, the child refused any nourishment and was content to suck its big toe. A senior disciple was immediately dispatched to verify the village gossip. He swore that it was not only true but that the child bore a striking resemblance to their erstwhile master. Since no one came forth to claim the child, proper applications were made by the ashram and the child was brought back to Nanjangud.

It was a miraculous event. People gathered in long lines to have darshan of the child and exclaimed about its resemblance to Pillai. It was only proper that the super yogi should return to his ashram as a child. It was god's will, god's symbolic gesture to believers; like Lord Krishna, Pillai had been returned on a leaf, naked as he went.

"My name is Prem Nath Yogi," announced the man who appeared at the ashram. He was very tall and wore a massive yellow turban wound up in the northern style. His beard, also long and tapered to a kneaded point, touched his stomach. He had eyes of an extraordinary size and he stared, as if by focusing he could unfathom a man's worst secrets. "I have been ordered to come here," he said and looked up at the sky.

Soon, Prem Nath Yogi had established his authority not only on the care and welfare of the child, but on the ashram itself. His manners and his haughty, all-assuming voice were heard everywhere. He set up new schedules for prayers and ordered the general conduct of the ashram, as if he had been appointed to take over Pillai's position. His voice was such that one obeyed it, not so much out of duty as out of sheer fear. No one dared to ask him who had ordered him here, for fear of being stared at so fiercely that one might disintegrate. His formidable build and intimidating manner kept everyone doing what he bid. If there were murmurs of protest, they went unheard.

Prem Nath Yogi took complete control over the child. The child was fed what he ordered and clothed and roomed where he wished—next to his own quarters. He was a fastidious man, a vegetarian, and a merciless practitioner of discipline. In fact, his meditations and prayer meetings lasted longer than Pillai's. As if there were any need to confirm his authority, on a holy day Prem Nath Yogi stood for the entire length of the auspicious phase on one foot in deep meditation, without moving a single muscle or hair. That same night, he called in the senior disciples and told each one exactly what he was thinking. Such divine perception after a strenuous yogic feat forever removed any misgivings. Prem Nath Yogi was accepted as the new director of the Paramayoga Ashram.

Rumors circulated that the new director was indeed a well-known North Indian yogi who had disappeared into the Himalayas for the last decade. His sudden appearance at Paramayoga Ashram must therefore be the intervention of Lord Shiva, who, despite assaults on Mount Everest by mortals, still reigned over it. Some wondered how he had survived in the Himalayas. People who had seen him taking baths in the Kabini River said that when he splashed his body, the water dashed away from his muscles as if it had hit rock.

The copper vessel looked like a toy in his hand. Prem Nath Yogi was not totally unaware of the speculations. One auspicious day, he called the disciples together. "Pillai Swami appeared to me," he began, but did not say where Pillai had appeared or how. "He asked me to go to Nanjangud and take over his functions. He said that he failed to walk on water because of a negative thought confluence in the gathering. In the form of this child, Pillai Swami will walk. Then he'll leave the child's body and return to heaven."

If one tries hard to find similarities to someone in the features of another, similarities will be found. But though the disciples wouldn't openly admit it, it took a lot of imagination to see Pillai in the child. Pillai had had rotten teeth made worse by chewing betel. Long hair had sprouted from his ears, and his nose almost looked into his mouth. But a child is a child, they reasoned. Given time, he too would look like his occupant. Anyway, if he succeeded in walking on water, who cared whether he looked like Pillai in his childhood or in his old age? There was something to the saying in English: *The child is the father of man.*

"The soul and body of this child have to be made astral. This is the only way that Pillai Swami can guide this child's body over water," said Prem Nath Yogi. And only he knew how to do this. The child was not only on a diet of secret herbs and roots, but Prem Nath Yogi allowed no one to witness how he trained the boy. Once, a disciple had peeped through the window to see the boy child walking in slow circles around Prem Nath Yogi on his hands. Thereafter, the window was closed and disciples were chastised. "You'll destroy the spiritual, as well as turn Pillai Swami into a ghost!" warned Prem Nath Yogi.

But the editor of the *Nanjangud Nutshell* commented in an editorial that Prem Nath Yogi had failed to walk on water in a much-publicized event in the northern city of Amritsar, and since then had disappeared. The boy child remained a mystery. "As long as there is spiritual static between religions, man will try to walk on water," was the conclusion. Of course, the editor was known to make facts out of rumor.

Tibetan refugees who had relocated in Somwarpet, sixty miles from town, began sporadically appearing and asking directions to the ashram. One disreputable looking Tibetan was seen conversing with Prem Nath Yogi. He became a familiar sight around the ashram, entering at sunset with a mysterious sack of goods that he exchanged for money.

"I need more money," said Prem Nath Yogi one evening after prayer. The night before, a strikingly beautiful woman had accompanied the Tibetan to the ashram gates where she waited while the Tibetan conversed with the yogi. The yogi had rushed disciples to prevent the woman from entering the ashram. Distressed, she had tried to plead with the ashramites; when they failed to understand her dialect, she had resorted to cradling her arms and rocking them to and fro, then pointing at her breasts. The Tibetan had saved them from embarrassment when he returned to hastily lead her away. At the prayer meetings, instead of concluding the hour with his usual philosophical discourse, the yogi remained in silent meditation, a gentle sadness playing across his face.

The child now sat next to Prem Nath Yogi during all prayers. Though he looked healthy, he also looked thinner. The yogi had forbid the ashramites from speaking with the boy. At the riverbank after his mornings with the yogi, the child was always anointed with potions and made to float on his back. He meekly obeyed every order the yogi gave him, though occasionally he was found fondly staring at the ice-cream cone in the hands of another when the yogi wasn't looking.

"Maybe the boy is tubercular," wondered one disciple, watching the boy sway unsteadily on his feet whenever a gust of wind swept over him. He'd flap his arms and try to fly, causing the ashram gathering to laugh.

"It's all these yogic exercises and secret herbs our master is feeding him."

"Those Tibetans are now bringing roots and herbs grown in the Himalayas that are supposed to have strange powers over gravity."

"I'm worried about his body. But if he's simply a mold for our Pillai master to accomplish the impossible, it should be all right."

"What if the mold gives up in spite of our Pillai being inside it?"

To that, they had no answer. They only hoped that their new master knew all the answers, but were afraid to ask. Though Prem Nath Yogi was stern in his supervision of the boy-child, he clearly doted over him. If the child moaned or cried in his sleep, Prem Nath Yogi was at his bedside within seconds. If the boy did not complete a routine, the yogi held him in his arms and gave him a massage. If he fainted, which was frequent, the yogi carried him over to the bed and sat beside him with a fan until he recovered. Though the yogi remained as stolid and inscrutable as ever, there were lines forming on his face, and he kneaded his beard with long, contemplative strokes.

At a prayer meeting, Prem Nath Yogi announced the event for which the entire ashram had been waiting. "Next month, on the first Friday, which is also the day our Pillai Swami died, at 8:00 P.M., when the full moon is completely out and glowing, the great spirit of our master will propel the body of the child over an expanse of water. Everyone in the ashram will commence purification ceremonies and individual meditation from now on."

Ponnsamy the ironsmith was to make a new drum with the wood of a neem sapling, and the water would be brought by the Tibetans from the source of the Ganges itself in the Himalayas. Everyone was to undertake fasts a week before the event, and the event was not to be publicized. Only the townsmen and other firm believers would be allowed to witness the event. The yogi forbid rumors, and specifically boycotted the presence of the *Nanjangud Nutshell*'s editor, a decision which sent the editor into a rage. But being a practical man, he refrained from letting his anger flow into his newspaper, hoping that his mended manners would please the yogi enough to let him in when the event took place. The child was guarded twenty-four hours a day, and the yogi spent many hours indoors with him. The boy-child became a holy presence at prayer meetings, for he was placed on a vow of silence. Thin as a wafer, he sat there with his eyes closed and his bony legs entwined in the lotus position. If he had levitated suddenly to the ceiling, it wouldn't have surprised anyone. The yogi carried him in and out as if he were a flower basket.

Suddenly, a series of unpredictable incidents took place a week before the child's yogic performance. Prem Nath Yogi had secretly instructed his senior disciples to bury himself alive next to Pillai's grave for three days so that he could receive whatever secrets the old master had to offer for the success of the event. On the second day, while Prem Nath Yogi sat in his six-foot-deep pit, covered by a corrugated iron sheet, the child fell into a delirium and kept asking for the holy water of Ganges, which was kept in the new drum. He started dehydrating so fast that the ashramites, fearing that he might fall into a coma or die, sought the town doctor, who immediately had the child transferred to the hospital and notified the inspector of police and the town magistrate of the boy's precarious condition. Police were posted to guard the child, and the nervous ashramites waited for their leader to emerge from his samadhi. Meanwhile, the nurses at the hospital placed the boy on intravenous feeding. The last hour of the third day, Prem Nath Yogi knocked from his underworld. Grateful disciples lifted him out. He looked unscathed after his ordeal. In fact, his face glowed, and he smiled with an expression of victorious understanding. But all this changed when he heard the news.

Instead of radiance, his face turned red and his nostrils flared.

"How dare, how dare," he raged, walking furiously round and round the prayer hall while the fasting disciples sat dumbfounded, wishing that they were thin enough to evaporate. Prem Nath Yogi had never been this way. In the early days of his arrival, when an urchin at the riverbank had thrown a stone at him, wounding him in the temple, Prem Nath Yogi had simply laughed. Later, sitting in the prayer meeting with his bandaged head, he had talked about the temptations of the material world and how the demons of base sense tease a yogi. "In each little boy, I see Lord Krishna. When Lord Krishna knows this, he tries to provoke me," he had said touching his head with reverence.

Accompanied by his followers, Prem Nath Yogi went to the magistrate's house to ask for the boy's release. A devout Brahmin, the magistrate had been offended that he was not to be at the yogic performance because of his public office.

"The boy is now under state protection. We cannot let him suffer or die," he said.

Prem Nath Yogi pleaded with him.

"There's nothing wrong with the boy's health. He always drank holy water at a certain hour of the night. His wish has been misinterpreted. The boy is now very holy, and the spirit of Swami Pillai sits inside him. Please let him be released for the yogic event. Afterward, if you wish, the boy can be fed whatever ordinary men eat."

The magistrate was obese and suffered from hypertension. He had just eaten his lunch, but he was already envisioning the plate of fried pakodas his wife would soon serve him. The smell of frying filled the house.

"Such a thing is not possible," he said, and rose from his chair.

Prem Nath Yogi's pleas with the police superintendent met with a similar refusal.

"I was looking forward to the event, but my hands are subordinate to law and order," the superintendent said. The inspector of police wouldn't even see the yogi.

When Prem Nath Yogi and his followers reached the hospital ward where the boy child was recuperating, a sympathetic crowd had gathered. But the news was bad. The child was now on bone marrow soup and egg custard, both of which he had asked for.

"He has been contaminated and impurified," said Prem Nath Yogi. "It will take many months to repurify his body and soul. Pillai Swami must have left his body and gone back to his burial in shame and dishonor."

The yogi visited the child daily at the hospital, and although he was downcast, he seemed to cheer up after spending an hour with the boy. The child had gained a few pounds and color had returned to his cheeks.

"There's only one thing to be done. I must perform the event," announced Prem Nath Yogi, and once again, he went to samadhi next to Pillai's grave. But this

time, it was going to be witnessed only by the ashramites. Everyone was sworn to the secrecy.

The event of course had to be postponed. The yogi
came out of his samadhi with the same expression he
had gone under. "Pillai is very upset and he refuses to
speak," he said about his conference underground.
Then he wanted to know how the boy was.

He fasted rigorously and shunned all human con-
tact. He had chosen the day of the half-moon, late in
the night. No time was appointed for the event. The
disciples were to keep a vigil.

"Some of you who are near siddhi may see it, others may not," was his verdict.

At the hospital, another story was unfolding. The
child was now completely normal and was allowed to
play with other town children. A rich town merchant
had applied for adoption. Prem Nath Yogi wandered
from one small bureaucrat to another.

"Unless you have papers to prove your guardian-
ship, we cannot consider your demands," they said.

Prem Nath Yogi looked haggard and beaten after his
fruitless wanderings. In the nights, he roamed the
empty prayer hall. His was the anguish of the bereaved. He had attained something, and now it had been
taken away from him. The vision of the evanescent boy
gliding like a swan over the inviolate skin of water was
now only a blur. He was lost without the prophecy of
his vision, so cleverly yet so inevitably snatched away
from him. His disciples sat outside in the dark, their
faces pale and bewildered like the faces of monks at the
feet of the dying Buddha in the frescoes. He was no

longer the tyrant of yogic discipline, but a humbled soul languishing in the sorrow of its failure. They heard him chant with great restraint, whispering to God to return his son. He had doted over the child so much, no wonder he called the boy his son. If, as he said, Pillai Swami had left the polluted body of the child, he hadn't entered Prem Nath Yogi's either, and Prem Nath Yogi sensed it. On the appointed night, the emaciated, agonized man climbed the ladder to the new drum and unceremoniously stepped over its Himalayan silence while the disciples moaned in yogic unison. He sank to the bottom as quickly as Pillai had. There was no need to retrieve him. He was a powerful swimmer.

"Pillai Swami wasn't with me," he remarked.

A few months later, Prem Nath Yogi appointed one of the ashramites as his successor. "The spirit of Pillai Swami will return the boy to your midst when he reaches enlightenment—the boy will renounce his wife and children and return to the ashram. Receive him then, and make him your new leader. When the time is ripe, he'll walk on water," he said.

Prem Nath Yogi disappeared from the ashram as mysteriously as he had appeared. He had left his meditation materials and what seemed to be a journal—wrapped and sealed with wax—for the child when he returned. A note said the yogi would come back, if he were alive, when the child was enthroned in Pillai Swami's position. Though the temporary head was kind and sympathetic, the ashramites missed the yogi. The disciple-in-charge felt the same way.

Meanwhile, only a few miles away in town, the child was absorbed in the material world. The true successor had grown fat sitting in his adopted father's grocery shop. He wore jewels on his fingers; there were rumors about his betrothal. He was indifferent to the ashram, though donations to it from the shop were generous and regular. His teeth had begun to rot, and long, immature hair sprouted from his earlobes. The ashramites watched him in secret anticipation, for he seemed to resemble Pillai Swami more and more each day.

3

NEITHER HERE NOR THERE

Bhat's Return

Bhat came to America to get a doctorate. Born to a wealthy merchant family, he didn't have to do anything. His father was an important ally of the ruling political party at home and could have had Bhat appointed to a well-paying job. In Iowa, Bhat met Becky, plain in a midwestern way, but her eyes reminded him of Cape Camorin, where the Indian Ocean meets the Arabian Sea. She was also the daughter of the dean. The first time they met on the tennis court, she asked, "How do you practice your religion in our country?" Weeks of tennis later, Bhat showed her how beside a boysenberry bush.

When Bhat wrote the eventual letter to his father, he praised Becky's indomitable quest for spiritual truth and her Indian-like modesty about her own physical beauty. Bhat's father had his doubts about the East successfully coupling with the West, spiritual truth or not, but shrewdly considered his son's prospects. After all, there were others in the Bhat extended family who had aspirations abroad. He consented to the marriage on the condition that they be remarried in the Hindu tradition later in India. Bhat didn't mind. He loved ceremonies as long as they were enjoyable. Bhat and Becky were married in Cedar Rapids. At the reception in the dean's house, the champagne was imported and his chairman assured him that everything had gone well with his orals.

Honeymooning in the Bahamas, Bhat woke up to the fact that Becky didn't care for Freeport luxuries. Once or twice she accompanied him to the gambling tables, but otherwise she preferred to stay in the room and read Gibran.

Bhat passed his written exams before the summer and was offered a position in the department. Becky thought they should go to India before he made a decision about his career. Bhat relished the idea of dazzling his old friends in Nanjangud with his American wife. Besides, the country had awakened to the tourist dollar. Western-style restaurants and beef had become popular. On the Air India jumbo, he was pleased at the improvements in decor and service. Maybe he ought to settle down in India. He could do so much for its universities with his Western training. Becky would be fascinated by India's history, and she would have a comfortable life with servants.

Becky didn't say much. She wanted to experience the country first. In a curious way, Bhat felt the same. He had changed, and he loathed his fellow countrymen on the jet with their thick accents discussing what they were taking home. At each airport they appeared to rush to the duty-free shops to gather more goods to sell for double in India. The aisles were jammed with their finds. For them, going home from the West was a return from an economic Disneyworld where, like wizards, they had wandered to purchase precious things to impress their brethren in the back country. And those who had spent some years in America had elaborate schemes on how to exploit their return, while their exteriors glowed with half-baked Westernism.

If he were to stay, perhaps there were ways in which he could reform their habits and minds. Perhaps he could enter politics and gain control over domestic affairs. Perhaps he could become an influential editor and write articles that would affect the way things were done. Who knew, he might even join the high ranks of Air India and mandate passenger behavior!

Becky woke him from his reveries. "The stewardess says only one bathroom is still usable, the one on the right side of Cabin C. The others are either filthy or broken down."

He should pass a law that would force all Indians who boarded jets to go through an orientation on how to use toilets. For now, Bhat decided he'd wait like the stewardesses for the next international airport.

In Bombay, everything measured small in his eyes, for he had become accustomed to divided highways and skyscrapers. His countrymen scurried around like dwarfs disturbed in their sleep. The airport was torn between modernization and the habits of countless generations unaccustomed to the jet age. The lounge resembled a railway waiting room, where pilgrims huddled on benches with their belongings tucked under their feet. Even his wealthy family looked like a *National Geographic* postcard. His haughty, aristocratic father occupied only half of his lavish silk shirt, which sagged under his armpits with huge arcs of sweat. His mother, despite the paan she had chewed for the occasion, smelled of sour buttermilk. His sister in her starched brocade moved stiff as a wooden puppet. Only the sight of Becky in the airport mirror rejuvenated his spirits. In the midst of Bhat's family, she swayed like a lotus just blossomed in the wind; and in the family car, huddled among his puny kinsmen, her hip gently rubbing against his thigh convinced him that with one powerful sweep of his arm, if he wanted to, he could transform the land.

Though Bhat didn't know how Becky felt, he hoped she would slowly adjust to the Hindu view of life. Becky was astounded by the country's contrasting riches and poverty. Beggars and emaciated children lined up for handouts on the sidewalks of luxury hotels like charred survivors of an explosion. The rich seemed to float over this misery in graceful strides or in air-conditioned cars. She could hardly eat anything at the restaurants. She saw the same tug between plenitude and hunger on the trains back to Nanjangud, her new family's ancestral home. Though her father-in-law had reserved an air-conditioned cabin, its tinted windows did not hide the agony of the beggars outside. Broken and mutilated women scraped her windows with their begging cups. Children with eyes like bomb craters hung onto the car's doors until the train gained speed and it was no longer safe for them to do so. After arriving in Nanjangud, she recovered enough to distribute American candy to servant girls, only to see them swallow the candy, tinfoil wrapper and all.

"How can you be so indifferent to such misery? How can you think of anything else when your conscience is bothering you about what's happening outside on the streets?" She protested when Bhat made advances under the mosquito curtain. Even the mosquitoes that she saw on the outside of the curtain seemed to be waiting for a leg or an arm to slip from under the tucked-in borders. She imagined that there might be even bigger carnivorous insects hiding in the thick darkness outside, waiting for her to grow careless in her sleep. In the humid night, sleep was not easy. When she finally fell asleep, she dreamed of having been bitten by some horrible insect that caused her thighs to swell to grotesque proportions, as the servant girls circled around, pointing at her.

Becky reluctantly consented to the second wedding only after Bhat assured her that he had prevailed over his parents to shorten it to the essentials. Bhat had to argue with his stubborn mother, who wanted the traditional three-day event in which the bride and bridegroom sat stiffly on wooden mats until the priests concluded that god, demons, and relatives had all been duly appeased. His mother surrendered only after he warned her of what such squatting could do to Becky's pelvis. That's why he had ordered a breakfast table and a commode. What he did not tell her about was

Becky's disaster with one of the heirloom saris in their
Indian-style lavatory. When half of it fell in, Becky
had chopped it off, sending the precious silk to the
nearest tributary of the Ganges.

Bhat's friends urged him to stay in India. His father
hinted at a future in politics. "With your qualifications
and my support, you'll in no time become a cabinet
member," he confided.

"We will build you a bungalow anywhere you like.
You can have a car and lots of servants. You can live
like a king," his mother said.

"What about my wife?"

"Oh, she'll adjust. Once she grows accustomed to
our ways, she'll never wish to go back."

Bhat was not sure about anything. He visited the
University, where all his old colleagues sat behind
red-and-black telephones that rarely worked. The
chairman of Humanities had invited him to address
an English literature class.

"Nothing too complicated. Something about T.S.
Eliot and the influence of Hinduism on his writings
would be nice," he added.

They were still in the dark ages, and ironically, they
liked it. He wondered about his own allegiances,
especially when Becky, during one of their frequent
fights, called him an opportunist. But everything he
had dreamed of reforming was too well settled in its
habits. The tiny Nanjangud Men's Club—in his
Indian days the wonderland he couldn't wait to
enter—was dimly lit and its lavatory reeked of urine.
Old civil servants played poker all evening and dirty

tumblers of coffee lined up on the veranda for days.
No one had heard of David Letterman. Other than
Bangalore City, some eighty miles away, the nearest
hamburger place was in Mysore, at a restaurant that
was open only during the tourist season. Though
everyone was polite to his white wife, there were hints
about his alienation, his Western ways and habits.
The land needed a Zapata who had his roots firm in
its soil, whose allegiances wouldn't be full of doubts.
It was hard for Bhat to follow the contorted logic of
his friends. When one of his friends, trying to impress
Becky, had said, "The glory of India becomes mani-
fest when you become an insider looking out, not vice
versa," Bhat had laughed hysterically, remembering
that just the previous day, Becky had seen a servant
boy peeping into the bathroom through the ventila-
tor. Yet as the days passed, it was Becky who seemed
to be growing more tolerant and accommodating. She
liked wearing the sari, though it kept slipping from
her shoulder like the straps of a camera. With the
persuasion of his sister, she joined the Mahila Samaj,
the town's association for women. She was in great
demand for lectures and demonstrations.

Becky no longer felt uncomfortable about the
country and its people. Instead, she felt that she could
do something to change it. She was flattered by the
tacit acceptance of her leadership by the women in
her family and at the Samaj. She felt comfortable in
the everyday cotton saris, and the rituals of attentive-
ness to the face and hands that Hindu women valued
so much. She began reading about the country's epics

and its spiritual mystics and leaders. Though she brought her own American brand of feminism to her involvement with the women's activities, she knew that everyone secretly admired her effortless adaptation to the Hindu way of life.

One Saturday, Bhat decided to take Becky to Bangalore and treat her to some of the delicacies the town was famous for. It was Ekadashi day, when the orthodox and the elderly fasted. But it was also the day on which those who didn't believe in such customs feasted out. As Bhat and Becky sat in a vegetarian restaurant, ready to dip into their dessert, an elderly man dressed in Binny's cotton pants and a close-collared shirt got down from his bicycle and approached them.

"I just saw you as I pedaled by this mahal," he said, joining his hands in a namaste. His sunken eyes swept over the plates and bowls of sweets. It was Bhat's old grammar school pundit. Bhat motioned him to sit and introduced him to Becky.

"I heard you had come back with family, but I was very busy with grading public examination papers," explained the pundit while Bhat mashed his jamoons into their thick syrup of honey, saffron, and goat cheese. The pundit went on apologetically, explaining how he had recognized Bhat from a distance even though the last time he had seen him was years ago. Bhat ate and made no move to offer anything to the pundit. Becky felt terribly uncomfortable and lit a cigarette. The pundit remembered incidents from Bhat's childhood when Bhat had been so shy and conservative that he wouldn't even touch his lunch if elders were around. The pundit had stopped at Bhat's lunch table one afternoon to ask him about his progress in other subjects at school. Bhat had stopped eating and his rice and chapatis had grown cold. Was the pundit trying to suggest something? Bhat wondered but did not ask. Instead, he called the waiter and ordered tea.

"I'd order some tea for you, too, pundit, but I know this is Ekadasi, and you being an orthodox Brahmin wouldn't touch a thing!" he said, winking at Becky.

The pundit beamed a weak smile, unable to say anything. On the half-eaten jamoons on Becky's plate, a fly had found the juiciest part and sat twirling its legs in triumph. Bhat knew that drinking a cup of coffee or tea on Ekadasi was not forbidden, even for the most orthodox. There were others in the restaurant who were dressed like the pundit.

"Say, pundit," taunted Bhat, "it must be torture for you to sit here suffering a stupid custom while others eat."

The pundit raised his hands and bowed.

"Well, sir, we are of the old, you know. Forgive me, I must go now. I only thought that I must stop by and greet you and your lovely wife."

"How could you!" yelled Becky, pointing a table-spoon menacingly at Bhat.

"Well, the bastard deserved it. Did you see the longing on his face? Why, if I were alone here and no-body he knew was around, he'd have gobbled every-thing in front of him, Ekadasi or no Ekadasi."

Bhat did not tell Becky the sweet exhilaration he had felt. Until now, in his mind, he had never been able to break out of some of the customs and behaviors he was brought up with. The pundit was one who had rejoiced in instilling some of them in the hearts and minds of schoolchildren, often with a sadistic test at lunchtime. Bhat needed to register on these old buzzards that he had changed, that the old did not cling to him like the sod on the pundit's sandals.

Bhat had instructed the travel agents to book their return passages when the Delhi Public Service Commission asked him to appear for an interview. The Indian airlines were on strike, so he asked Becky to accompany him to the interview on the train. Becky had had enough of trains. Besides, she had committed herself to be Mistress of Ceremonies at the silver jubilee of the Samaj. The Delhi trains took a week to reach their destination. At the interview, the commission was more interested in his American self than in his candidacy. His father had warned that political unrest was growing at the capital, where some of his enemies were gaining power.

"Our salaries are low compared to your universities in the u.s. Our educational standards are also low. We are slowly de-emphasizing English studies, and we wonder how you would fit in," commented one of the members who had shown interest in him.

Bhat had already seen the effects of such de-emphasis. The popular texts with commentaries that were in use were atrociously out of date. One widely used text for graduate studies, prepared by an Indian scholar, was full of errors.

"Eventually, all English books will be in translation and we will have no comparative literature in your sense of the term," was the prophecy of the commission.

At Nanjangud railway station, his family was in great panic.

"Your wife has left us. We do not know where she is at the present. I have cabled the American Consulate about her disappearance," said his father, wiping his forehead with his stained shoulder towel. While Bhat had still been on the return train, the rival political faction suffered a no-confidence motion, dooming his father's political allies. With Becky's disappearance, Bhat's family was dealing with two calamities.

"You wouldn't believe how Indian she has become since she joined the Mahila Samaj," said his mother. "She has taken to praying our way and reading our books. When the guru came, she was the bold one who confronted him for days at prayer meetings with deeply philosophical questions. She visited him twice at the Traveler's Bungalow. We suspect she has run away with him."

Bhat had heard of the Poona Guru, who had a large number of American disciples.

Bhat wrote to the American Council in Madras. "From what we have gathered, your wife is with the Poona Guru. They're traveling to pilgrimage centers. We received a call from her the other day. She said that she was fine," wrote back the Consul.

There was a telegram from Becky which simply said: SAFE. LETTER FOLLOWS. The letter came three days later. It had the Arsikere postmark but no return address.

Dearest Bhat,
An enchanting thing happened to me while you were away in Delhi. Swami Gurunath appeared in the Samaj and changed my entire conception of the Self! All our lives we sit and while away Time waiting for a better tomorrow; When all our todays eventually amount to a No Tomorrow, we weep for our waking. I'm safe. Do not worry about me. There are three Germans and an American Professor with us and we'll be traveling thru Cape Camorin onward to Sri Lanka. Guess what else! He fasts on Ekadasi! Don't do anything foolish. I'm writing to father.

Yours, Becky

Under P.S. she had hastily scribbled, "Oh, I almost forgot. I'm pregnant! How exciting! I do want our child to be born in God's country."

In a pamphlet of the guru that she had left behind, it said that all mortals are expatriates of the true country of spirit. But where between Nanjangud, India, and Pella, Iowa, was Becky's idea of God's country? Bhat wandered in the house like a lost man. He was somewhat relieved when his sister mentioned that Becky had been throwing up a few days before the guru arrived.

"You should've married an Italian girl like our prime minister's son did, or an English girl. They're more reliable," said his father.

When the Public Service Commission expressed its regrets, the family knew that Bhat had to return to the States. His mother entertained hopes that she might be able to persuade her son to marry an Indian, but after a heroic attempt to arrange his meeting with a Bangalore silk merchant's daughter who swore by her Murjani's, she gave up.

"So, you've decided to go back! What a pity. All our brains are draining away to the outside," said the customs officer, who wore a soiled white shirt with the rusty insignia of Indian lions on his shirt pocket. The late-night 747 out of the country was full of Americans returning. The only Indian family on board was tucked away in a corner in the next cabin. His companions in row 23 were glad to see him.

"You talk just like us but with a more distinguished voice," commented the blonde from Kansas. She worked in bars and took acting lessons. Her eyes were azure as the Caribbean.

After dinner, as the huge jet purred over the Atlantic in the cloudless night, Bhat sauntered over to the kitchen and, commanding his best Indian pidgin, said to the sleepy-eyed blue sari, "You got somethink thrust kwenching for Hindu & Kompany?" The stewardess smiled as she reached for the glasses. Bhat, expertly balancing whiskeys in both hands, waltzed back to his seat softly whistling a Sinatra tune. Kansas beamed. He kissed her gently on the brow as he had seen his father kiss the holy cow.

Selves

A man ought to keep his private life to himself and ought not to be judged for his grandness as a public figure if he indeed was one. Remember Lingappa, the "one-rupee-notice lawyer?" He used his matrimonial connection to become a judge. When he was still a bachelor, he lived in his dismal bachelor quarters on Ballal Street and scurried to the courtrooms in his rain-soaked black coat like a mouse in despair. Even the milkwoman's cow used to look the other way. Now, he drives his shiny black car through the main street, honking at every lane to make sure everybody sees him. All the milk cows on their daily rounds have forgotten what he was before, and gaze at him with admiration. Ramayya's white one, which has the fattest udder in the entire town, moos after him and flaps her tail with pleasure at his purring exhaust. I don't know if Ramayya's cow has fallen for the car or if she appreciates Lingappa's prominence. I might even dismiss this as a quadruped's inability to have foresight or hindsight, but even our townsmen have forgotten everything about Lingappa the bachelor lawyer, who for one rupee would lie and lampoon the judges until he got his way. He hasn't changed much. Now he lampoons himself, if you ask me, when he looks down upon other unfortunate members of his profession who are still struggling to keep their starved bodies ticking under their graduation coats.

Our English professor was nothing until he went abroad on a Rotary scholarship. Now whenever someone needs an English-speaking master of ceremonies, he is the star. His English hasn't changed, nor his accent, but everybody thinks he's superior to other local English-speaking luminaries because he has been to the West and has studied among men of superior language and tastes. Does having a superior language make the West superior in character? I agree that English adds class to our tongue, enhances our public image, but does it really cure lisping, as our Ayurved pundit claims? He says speaking English regularly for half an hour each day will strengthen tongue muscles, rebuild posture, and even improve one's complexion. He makes every one of his seven children recite Pope's "The Rape of the Lock" loudly every day before the sun sets. You can hear them on your evening walk. From a distance you can't be certain whether they are chanting Pope or moaning the "Rape," but look at the grades they've been making at school! I have my doubts about their complexion, though. I bet that the pundit feeds them one of his special potions to make them glow in their cheeks.

The British, when they ruled our country, gave us fine examples of how to keep our public and private selves separate. We never knew what our viceroys or generals were like in their bedrooms, but we knew how good they were in their offices. If there were some stories on who did what on a shikari with whose memsab, I feel they were the result of vicious gossip created by illiterate native servants who had no sense or understanding of the divisions in life. It was the British who gave us the beauty of a statement like "None of your business." It acts like a quick whiplash on the nose of a poking bore who has no right to someone else's privacy. Alas, even with such good teachers and over three centuries of lessons, we Indians haven't learned a blessed Western thing. We imitate when it serves our purpose—like a cur trying to bark like a bulldog—then we fall back to our national character and hide our conniving and gossiping selves behind our public importance.

Varadraj, our town dentist, may have been an exception. He was a good dentist, as good as any trained native ones come, and he was the only one in Nanjangud. His private and public lives were an open book. He knew enough English, though his wife from Kollegal was illiterate and had her reputation for screaming and assault with deadly pots and pans firmly established. He worked miracles on a passing Scotsman's molar and was invited to England for further training. He stayed in England for two years and when he returned, he was a changed man. His Indian dress had changed to British, he spoke through a pipe, and wore a Scottish plaid beret. He changed his business sign to English, renovated his office, installed shining new equipment. He arrived punctually at nine in the morning, whether he had patients waiting or not. But what was really different was his insistence on speaking only in English. At first, everyone thought it was just an affliction that would pass away like the common cold, but they were wrong. Varadraj did not mind if others spoke in Kannada, but his answers were all in English. It annoyed everybody, but decaying teeth do not wait for the return of the native language, so his patients learned to put up with English. Besides, Varadraj's assistant Vasant helped as a translator. Varadraj's friends at the club all spoke English, so it did not bother them. They said he had developed a Scottish pitch. Varadraj did another odd thing. He filled the walls of his office with shelves of books on literature and poetry, but very few on dentistry. I think it befitted a man like Varadraj, who was a voracious reader given to silent gazes at the horizon when he was not working. Anyway, nothing much has changed in the art of dentistry for new books to be written about. Through the centuries, it has always been drill and hammer, drill and hammer.

The real problem was Varadraj's wife, who doggedly refused to change or to adjust to his new style of life. Varadraj moved to his living room, where he spent his evenings alone listening to English music. Joseph of the Traveler's Bungalow and his bicycle became a common sight on the compound of Varadraj's house. Dogs gathered in the mornings to poke and fight in the garbage bin outside, where Joseph threw away his lonely master's chicken bones after a night of late repast. One day, after a fiery onslaught on her husband with a silver vessel, her wedding gift, Varadraj's wife left for Kollegal. The entire compound had heard her screaming the previous night, though Varadraj had turned up his music to muffle the fracas. Joseph says that when she finally succeeded in landing one of her throws on Varadraj's wrist and slashed his palm, all the gentle dentist uttered was "Poor, brazen soul."

But as I said earlier, Vandraj had adopted the English manner. He never talked about what was going on. When his wife left, he continued his public life as if she had never existed. He spent more of his private time at the club, but that was not unusual since he was president and was supervising construction of the new tennis court. Even his best friends couldn't get a word out of him. Varadraj would have said "None of your business" if they had persisted. He was seen with a book in his hands, walking by the Kabini River, reciting things unto himself. Later, he would stay in one of the balconied rooms at the Traveler's Bungalow. Joseph transported Varadraj's music equipment to and fro.

Then the Hills arrived in Nanjangud. Mr. Hill had sold his cardamom plantation in Coorg and was on holiday. Mrs. Hill, a quiet, raven-haired woman in her thirties, was a writer. Varadraj did some dental work on both of them, and they became friends. They dined together at the Traveler's Bungalow, and on days when Varadraj had his handful of patients, they came to his house and spent the evening. Passersby on the road could hear Mrs. Hill's birdlike twitter punctuating the sound of violins and piano.

Varadraj regained his spirits rapidly, and hastened the completion of the tennis courts. On their inauguration, Mrs. Hill cut the green ribbon and there was an exhibition match between Mr. Hill and Varadraj. Though Varadraj lost, he got more cheers from the ladies. Only the natives gossiped about Mrs. Hill and Varadraj.

Then suddenly Varadraj's wife returned with a maid and a whole new batch of vessels. Varadraj was at his office when she arrived, and Joseph came running to tell him the news. Varadraj went pale in his face. No one knows if Mrs. Hill was at his house, but everybody heard a great deal of clattering and a distinctly gentle voice that took control of the situation. Varadraj did not come to his office the following Monday, the first day he had ever missed. On Tuesday, Nanjangud bid farewell to the Hills with a reception at the club. Mrs. Hill was garlanded with flowers, and she read a poem she had written while in Nanjangud. There were tears in Varadraj's eyes.

If a change had occurred in Varadraj's life, it was certainly unnoticeable at first. He drank a little bit more and took his meals at the Traveler's Bungalow. Varadraj seemed content with being a recluse. But a month later, he announced at a club meeting that he would be opening an office in Bangalore and until such time as he would have a replacement for his profession in Nanjangud, he'd spend one week each month there. Everyone protested, but there wasn't much anybody could do.

Murugesh is now our new dentist. Varadraj finally left Nanjangud five weeks ago. His wife and her brother are trying to sell the property. Mrs. Varadraj's brother goes about town telling everyone how Mrs. Hill stole his sister's husband and all her wedding jewelry. Such acts would be normal here, even if no foreign woman were involved. I know of extended families where the wives of some steal from the wives of others and blame it all on a servant or a distant relative. Foreigners, especially if they are not coming back, are heaven-sent for these greedy people. Mr. Basudev's son came back from the United States with an American wife. Mr. Basu had them wait in Bombay so he could go there and chase the girl away. When he came back with his "singularized" son, he spent weeks telling everyone in town how much money he had to pay the American girl to free his son from bondage. I know what Mr. Basudev did with all that money in Bombay!

Many of us here miss Varadraj. He tried not to mix his skill in extraction of teeth with the turbulence in his private life. The new dentist, Murugesh, has established himself here, but that is where the similarities tragically end. Murugesh has three daughters and a wife no different from Mrs. Varadraj. Other than easy money and the prospects of finding rich husbands for his daughters, the only thing that interests this dentist is his predecessor, whose name he ruins with a renewed fervor every time someone complains of his own shoddy work.

Varadraj now lives in Wales with Mrs. Hill, Murugesh says. They've built a cottage with the money they stole from Varadraj's Indian wife. He says that Mrs. Hill is a Welsh witch who tried to poison her husband and was caught and imprisoned. Murugesh chews on his internal jealousy until the rot settles in his teeth. His wife has no sense of scruples or dignity, either. The last time she had a fight with her husband, she sat on the front steps of her house and called everyone passing by to come and hear her complaints. At least Mrs. Varadraj did her thing indoors. One Friday, there were more people gathered in front of Murugesh's house than there are in front of the Magistrate's court on a criminal case. Eventually the magistrate had to send his wife to calm the woman and take her inside. Murugesh stayed in his office cooking up his own tirade against his wife.

The new tennis court has become a morass of holes and cracks ever since Varadraj left. All his books of poetry and literature are now at the Samaj library, as he had wished. The poem that Mrs. Hill read at the farewell hangs on the club's wall, tenderly framed. I tell you, Varadraj tried, then left. From this town, self-respect and dignity left with him.

Protector of Dogs

For someone who loved dogs, Bhavani knew nothing about them. She had adored the dogs her parents reared, the ones she grew up with, but to her dogs were sacred. They were protected by Lord Brahma. To kill or maim one was to inherit his wrath. It would take many repentant births to cleanse oneself of such sin.

This morning the dew clung to the white and blue phlox under the bedroom window. A light wind played on the mellowed leaves of the elm by the driveway of her new house. Ever since she left India, she had lived in apartments where she was her own prisoner and guard. Even after marrying Greg, they'd had to live in one until Greg finished his doctorate and found a position. This was her very first home, with a front and a fenced back. Bhavani was thirty-six, and time had done little to coarsen her gazelle-like agility or grace. She was small boned and her eyes were dark. She wore the Indian sari or the American slacks with equipoise. She had seen Greg to the door this morning to share a ride with a neighbor. It had been three weeks ago, driving back from a party, that she had hit the dog. It was a stray mongrel. The police were very sympathetic.

"You did it a favor. It was starving."

(Starving like its brethren in the old country.) She had insisted on bringing the corpse home. She dug a grave close to the bedroom window, shaping the hole into a crib with her hands. She slashed her feathered pillow and made a bed. She covered the mongrel with a piece of silk she had been saving for a blouse. Greg thought the whole thing was crazy. She was the daughter of a man who reared magnificent hounds, who fed the less fortunate dogs of her town every Saturday in charity and had built a clinic for their care. When Greg was away, she poured milk over the grave for seven days.

Since the accident, whenever she turned on the TV, she saw dogs. Today it was the British trainer. "You must show the dog that you love it," the trainer said as she made the various thoroughbreds of movie stars obey. The dead mongrel had been handsomer than any of the so-called stars. One of its parents must have been a hound. An Englishman who had courted her had had a hound that looked like the mongrel. He had let her christen it Lord Brahma and was offended when she thwarted his advances next to the stream of gliding swans on his estate. That was long ago and far away. Bhavani caressed her shoulders absentmindedly. She was soft and her clear brown skin was warm. Tonight they were throwing a party for Greg's colleagues. She decided to wear something especially Indian.

"We call this a dog necklace. I know it sounds funny, but these miniature gold coins have faces if you look under a lens," she explained to Kathy, who was researching Hindu women. The discussion turned to Hindu dogma, TV adaptations of Kipling and Forster, and whatever had happened to Satayjit Ray since his popular *Apu* trilogy.

Jean, married to an anthropologist, moved over to tell of her husband's discoveries. "In Malaysia, dogs are believed by many tribes to be ancestral reincarnations. Some witch doctors keep a family of dogs and will not travel without them. In Kuala Trengganu, we heard of a witch doctor who consults his dead dog before he prescribes any medicine."

Bhavani confided to Jean of her own infatuations. In her family, dogs were treated as members of the family. When her favorite had died from poisoning, she had asked her father not to bring any more into their household. To Bhavani, the dog had been her brother, the only son to the family. For the rest of the evening, Bhavani sat by herself. She watched the party as if from a cave, moving only when she needed to, offering appropriate nods or smiles to those who sought them. It seemed as if everyone needed only limited gestures of affection from her, like a pat on the head. Then they'd saunter off, happy and encouraged. Bhavani's hand instinctively reached for a familiar ear beside the chair. She caressed it until her fingers traced the thick curls around its neck and she could feel the moist breath on her nails. When the mongrel started licking her hand, she awoke with a start.

"Sorry, did I scare you?" It was Jean. Everyone had left except for Jean and her husband, who was in the kitchen with Greg. Bhavani turned on the TV and watched Johnny Carson say, "We'll be right back!"

Later that night, when Greg sent his hands on familiar explorations, she did not respond; instead, she lay there imagining herself as an arid prairie. She saw Greg hovering over a distant bush, inexplicably clawing for something. He worked furiously, and then collapsed. She meant to call his name until the dark prairie echoed with her trembling voice.

"Are you pregnant, by any chance?" asked Greg the next morning. She shrugged her shoulders. That was enough answer for Greg. He kissed her good-bye and left. Greg was very practical. If one got sick, one went to a doctor and then to a pharmacist. He had his own burdens to carry. This was their first year, and Greg had to make the right impression. His tenure depended on it, and on the Valium he kept within reach, like cigarettes.

She must do penance; not any act of penance, but one of which her father would approve. She needed a temple priest to chant and her dead father to ask forgiveness of the gods. That was the only proper ritual. No, she wasn't silly or illogical. She didn't need a tradesman of the psyche to analyze her wanting or to interpret her soul's mystical hum until it was dry of sap. When the sun broke through the low-lying clouds, Bhavani noticed the doghouse by the back fence under a heap of leaves. She swept the roof with her palms. The roof was slippery. Leaf mold clung to her nails and hair. The inside of the house was caked with dirt and pulpy stems. She worked on it all afternoon. She got on her knees to enter the small arched opening. It was warm inside, and as she moved, the splintered sides of the boards scraped her sides. When she was finished, she turned and sat inside, just in time to catch a cardinal, out on a brief respite, dart radiantly across her backyard.

It snowed heavily the next morning. Bhavani spent the afternoon watching the doghouse, waiting for the snow to stop. She'd paint the inside in bright lemon with dark orange for the trim. The baby quilt she had picked up at a yard sale would fit nicely. But something still wasn't right. She put on an old pair of jeans and a sweater. She gave the house a push. It wouldn't budge.

Bhavani decided she'd wait for Greg. Greg burst in with his own news.

"I got a grant to do research for two weeks in London," he said as he took off his hat and overcoat. He wanted to eat right away and excused himself after dinner. She could hear him busily typing the forms he had brought back from the office. The house filled with the aroma of his newfound pipe, which he scarcely took from his mouth. It was a restless night for her. She dreamed of walking under the awnings of strange storefronts, afraid to ask directions to her own home, which she had just left.

At breakfast, when she asked Greg to give her a hand to move the doghouse, he said "sure" unhesitatingly and got up. He was so cheerful and preoccupied he almost carried the doghouse all by himself backward to the spot next to the bed of phlox. She waited for Greg to ask her why she wanted it moved to such an odd spot. She opened her mouth to speak, but Greg had run back to the vacant patch and was looking for something.

"What is it?" she asked instead.

"Nothing," answered Greg without turning. "I dropped my pipe someplace here."

On the way to the airport, Greg suggested various things that she might do while he was away. She listened. He didn't notice the stains on her pants or the scratches on her elbow and forearms.

"The doghouse is now over the mongrel's grave," she said abruptly when Greg paused to light his pipe.

"That's why you wanted it moved! I didn't think of that," he replied.

"Does it bother you?" she asked

"Not if it doesn't bother you. I want you to be happy," he answered.

She couldn't remember the drive back. She parked in front of the village restaurant at the shopping center. It was too early for the luncheon crowd, and the empty chairs sat staring at each other in their pact of silence. What were these blind veterans of obedience thinking? Once upon a time, they had been trees holding their heads high in a giddy cluster of defiance. Look at them now! Chopped, broken down, sliced, they squatted oddly, loners in any row of formation, always with that orphaned gape of sadness.

"Our special today is clam chowder and sole almondine," said the pubescent waiter in the green apron. He wore sneakers, and a button on his shirt was missing. "Would you like to order now or can I get you a drink from the bar?"

"What is your name?" Bhavani asked, leaning on the glass top and bringing her face close to his.

"I beg your pardon!"

"Your name!"

"Tom."

"Tom what?"

"Tom Bedlington!"

Bhavani threw the napkins from the table high up in the air and laughed. Tom caught one of them.

"I'm sorry, madam. Is there anything I can get you? A glass of water maybe," Tom awkwardly whispered, uncertain whether the lady was already drunk.

Bhavani grabbed Tom by his neck. Tom grinned and blushed, trying gently to free himself.

"Let's go out," whispered Bhavani in his ear.

Tom reeled backwards.

"Come, Bedlington. Let's ride in my car!"

Tom dropped the empty tray tucked under his shoulder and ran.

Bhavani walked to the bar and asked for a double vodka. She drank until she was half drunk and tears blinded her. She raced home in her Volkswagen. She had left her coat in the restaurant, nameless and hanging as she had found it in a flea market in a place more distant and lost in memory. The milkman had left the extra jug at the doorstep. She unbuckled her white sandals and unplugged the telephone. She locked the house from the inside. Everything took a long time, as if her body had fallen into a suspension, as if in a few moments when she walked into the backyard, the expectant wind would lift her and hold her in its inviolate arms. She picked up the blanket and the jug of milk. This time she knew how to ease herself in without a scratch. Only her naked legs, wrapped with the blanket, stuck out on the hard frosted grass.

Encounter

When the dust of hot, arid days rises all afternoon, when the sun mellows and birds seek trees in droves, their frantic cackle drowning human noises in the bazaar, the hovering dust creates mirages in cobbled alleys, in front of fruit shops ablaze with gas lamps and bangle stalls with their myriad glass loops tied to the roof. The dust is everywhere and the horizon is so thick with it that the descending sun is enveloped in a monk's saffron. The clouds take the shapes of mythic hunters and the hunted. Shadows of gold and ochre follow them. The birds, now settled, find it hard to stay down. They flutter and chase each other in small circles around their perches, cacophonous or in ecstasy, as the dark descends. There are reflections in water puddles as bicyclists splash through them. Pedestrians whom you passed a moment ago seem to reappear in front of you with sudden familiarity. You do not know them, and they aren't apparitions come to haunt you in the dusty twilight.

I was twenty-seven when I left India for good. Since then, I've steered a new course in my life. I've married and have three children under the age of ten. Though India is always on my mind, there's no link that connects the sudden stop my life came to there and my new self. I leaped from one life to another, and in between I left nothing but a vacuum. Only imagination and memory, when I need them, act as my bridges. Thus, whenever I go back to India, I'm a stranger wandering almost invisibly in familiar neighborhoods. I recognize every tree, river, palace, every sunset, every night of the full moon. But friends or relatives stumble in surprise at my familiar ways of greeting them. I explain, identify, and affirm. We look at each other through our gray hair, our wrinkled faces, our ravaged bodies for a semblance of that once-upon-a-time when we were insepar-able. Something quietly fathomed clears the film in our eyes and we smile, embrace, or shake hands. But the sudden intimacy is unreal. We remain at large, distant and clothed by our separate worlds. We know that the bonds we shared while growing up do not unite us anymore. We do not represent ourselves.

One afternoon I saw an astrologer under a tree. He was the type who reads the palms of transients and villagers, chooses an auspicious day for an occasion, blesses an event for a fixed, competitive fee. I was shabbily dressed, my hair was disheveled, and my feet inside my Indian sandals were dusty. I hadn't used my deodorant, and I carried a soiled handkerchief tied around my neck like any other hardworking Indian employee of low means.

The astrologer was duped. He asked me to pick up his four cowrie shells and throw them on his mat. I shook them vigorously and let them roll. The numbers ran even. He held my palm and read my story: I was a public servant. I was educated and led a comfortable life with a wife and two teenage daughters. In the recent past, things had been difficult. I was worried about my health, which had suffered a setback. I was also worried about the future of my daughters. My recent illness had left its scars. If I took care of my mental and physical health, I might live to my late sixties or even seventies. My wife was a strong influence over my well-being, since she did not belong to my caste and brought some non-aligned planets in conjunction. My wife was probably a Muslim.

I thanked him and left a five-rupee note on his mat. His handwritten sign advertised his fee as two. He was startled at my generosity and rose to his feet to thank me. My Western gesture had given me away. There was a look of awe on his face. He stood there watching as I mingled with the evening crowd on the street. Where was this man whose life continued the way the astrologer had read it? Had my life continued here without me? I wanted to see the man who had continued it, wanted very much to meet his teenage daughters. If his illness had anything to do with the heart, I wanted to apprise him of the wonderful progress made in the West.

I could tell him the diet I followed, the pills I took, and the way I overcame my fear of bypass surgery. I could send him drugs that weren't available in India or were too expensive for him to buy. I could send him my own! Then I thought of his wife. I imagined her in her Muslim ways. She would have found a compromise between her faith and his. They had formed a bond of love that prevailed over their religious differences. Surely they loved each other and endured their sufferings on the strength of their love. If she were a Muslim and he a Hindu, their sufferings must have been plenty. If I had stayed back in India, would I have married a Muslim?

The bazaar was filled with its evening traffic. Some of the shops lacked electricity, and gas lights blazed in them, creating a haze around oranges stacked in pyramids. A thirtyish woman in a hooded sari caught my attention. She was standing in front of a bangle stall, trying various types of bangles. Her face was partly hidden by the sari and the shadows that the lamps cast. Something compelled me. I was embarrassed at being in front of a bangle stall without a woman accompanying me, but I took heart in the ivory and sandalwood carvings the shop also displayed. The owner was busy with the woman and ignored me. A boy assistant came to my aid. I was glad. I examined cheap miniatures while my ears remained glued to the symphony of bangles as the woman tried them on. I surreptitiously moved closer, as close as I could stand to her without causing any commotion.

Her perfume was familiar. Something I could not name. I could not remember where I had first smelled it. The nails on her left fingers were painted in magenta. They were long, beautiful, and again, familiar. I felt a shiver, for I thought that those fingers, as they paused over the tabletop, knew that I was looking at them. They nudged each other, and each one of them observed me. I began to sweat. Her hand was close to mine, and though I busied myself with ivory elephants, gods, birds on branches, letter openers, I felt a powerful urge to grab it. I had the assistant parade everything he had on the shelves and at some point switched to speaking in English. The assistant had figured me out and was smiling as he would at any gullible foreigner. He didn't mind my quick glances at the woman, as if he understood the turmoil within me. Suddenly the woman became conscious of my proximity and of my hand reaching for hers in violent familiarity. She pulled her hand away and tugged her sari over her head more tightly. She whispered something to the shop owner, picked up her handbag, and left.

Mesmerized, I followed her, craning my neck over the bobbing heads of shoppers, through parked bicycles and squatting vegetable sellers. She walked briskly. She knew her way, and her body moved inside her sari with a panic the folds did not betray. She sensed me behind her. I could smell her fragrance on my cheek as if she had touched me. It was in my collar, in my fingers as I wiped my brow. I knew her and I wanted to hold her and say, "It's only me!" But I could not remember her name! How could I forget the name of my beloved, my only love! I tried frantically to recall her name to my lips before she disappeared forever. The increased pace at which I followed her suddenly caught up with me, and a sudden pain of angina shot through my chest.

I had to stop. The pain was too intense. I groped for my pills and rolled one to my palm. I swallowed it. I put the cap back on and shoved the bottle into my pocket. The pill caught in my throat. I bought an orange, tore open its skin, and squeezed the juice into my mouth. The sweet juice ran all over my beard and through my fingers. I had lost her. I did not know where I was. I looked around and saw myself in the middle of a strange place, surrounded by people who spoke a strange dialect. All the signboards in front of shops were in a language I could not recognize. Was I having a heart attack? I had forgotten the direction from which I had entered the bazaar and which way I was headed. I stopped a stranger. "Please," I whispered in my hoarse voice. "Can you tell me which way is . . ."

He asked me in English. "Are you all right? Which hotel do you want to go?"

I could not tell him. He mentioned several hotels. I could not recognize any one of them.

"I think you must be staying in Métropole. That's the only decent hotel for foreigners here," he said, convinced of my stature. He pointed me the way. "Don't worry," he shouted after me. "You'll be fine once you get back. It's all this heat and confusion!"

A flock of egrets rose sharply into the air from a low-lying branch as a turning car honked at my intrusion.

I staggered out of its way. The car slowed down. The driver rolled his window down to ask me if I was all right. In the backseat sat the woman from the bangle shop with two teenage girls.

The guard at Métropole gave me his stiff military salute. The key with the long red plastic tag told me my room number. I had entered familiar territory, and with the drink I ordered to be sent to my room, things began to settle in my mind. I took my pulse; it was normal. The angina attack had disappeared completely. When I turned off the lights, the dark that enveloped me didn't feel right. I didn't belong here in this dark. I had a home to go back to, a home whose dark soothed me to sleep. If I had stayed in India and continued the unforked life the astrologer had seen in my palm, perhaps I would have been the driver of that car. I'd have been that Muslim woman's husband, and those two teenagers in the backseat would have been my daughters. But this darkness in the hotel room was neither. It was an unfamiliar middle, an illusory passage that connected me to what I could've been, nothing else.

shubhamastu

PR
9499
.3.S45
S27
1998

GOSHEN COLLEGE - GOOD LIBRARY

3 9310 01054750 1